Fright

Merry F*cking Christmas

Shelby Manuel

Table of Contents

Author's Note

Hello, my dark romance lovelies.
If you're looking for a book with a healthy balance of plot
and spice, I have other books published to suggest to you,
but this series is <u>not</u> about balance.
It's about the smut.
Dark, kinky smut to be exact.

Merry Fucking Christmas isn't about celebrating the
holidays with family and friends, these stories are filled with
morally grey men that will do anything to get what they want.
And what they want is their dangerous, strong, unhinged
women.
Mix that with a healthy dose of violence, and you have my
dark mirror of a wholesome Christmas tale.
If you have triggers, I've listed them extensively at the
front of the book.
Stay smutty, and mentally safe.

Want a few more stories to escape into?

Merry Fucking Christmas
Anthology Series - Extra spicy novellas
Christmas Guest
Christmas Dare

Agency Soldiers
A dark, stalker romance series
Flower's Beast
Moon's Ghost

Factions of Red River
An interconnected, dark, dystopian romance series
Fog
Wasteland
Bones

Why have one morally disturbed stalker chasing, when you can have three?

Chapter One
Micah

"When are we taking out this sick piece of shit?" I twist my switchblade in my hand before trailing it over my knuckles.

"Put it away. We need to blend." Declan snaps his hand to cover mine that's gripping my knife, but I don't let go, debating how furious he'd be if I rammed it into his shoulder right now. "He doesn't have an address listed, so this is the only place we know he'll be." He raises his brows to warn me to calm down as he and I share a hostile glare where he waits to see if I'll snap before Cain's chuckling distracts me.

"We're gonna get him, Micah, just give it twenty more minutes. This pig thinks he can get away with touching kids." Cain tightens his jaw and quickens his tapping on the table before smoothing back into his pleasant façade. "I don't care where we do it. I'm happy as can be to take *Santa* out this year." He gives us a wink with a smirk as he leans his elbow back on the table, but his hands are flexed so hard his knuckles are white. His entire body is as primed and ready to rip our target apart as mine is. He's just hiding it better than me.

I try to conceal my murderous scowl when I remember we're surrounded by *people*. We need to get this the fuck over with. I can't be out in the wild this long.

"Did it have to be at a damn mall though?" I snarl under my breath as I jerk my head at some idiot who stares at us for too long. *Pay attention to your kid who's drowning her doll in the fountain instead of worrying about me and my knife, you lazy fuck!* I

1

scream at him in my head, hoping my glare relays my message.

"Close your eyes and focus on how you're going to make him suffer." Declan slowly releases my knife and taps the side of my head to see if I'm in control. "The Santa pictures should be done soon. Then we'll follow him back to wherever he lives and finish him." He sits back, trying to seem relaxed, but his stiff posture and deepening scowl give him away.

As the shoppers skim their eyes over us, they probably can't tell that we introduce people to their last moments for work and for fun, but everyone seems to understand that we like our space. The mall is overflowing, as consumers mindlessly march here during the holidays, but the tables around us stay empty, causing a few people to eat standing up. They all want us to leave as much as I want to go.

Following Declan's command as I've been trying to do more often, I tuck my knife back into my jacket and close my eyes. Even though this is the worst spot for me to be, I'm thrilled when we're hired to take out scum like this. We usually do jobs like this for free, but the client paid extra for our target to *suffer*. The guys are releasing my reigns when we finally get him. I can get creative.

I think I'll start by slicing off his fingers. Maybe I'll take a few of these salt packets and rub it into his wounds before cauterizing them. I don't want him to bleed out too soon. But maybe he'll pass out. Shit. I hate it when that happens. I bet we have a shot of adrenaline in the trunk though. And when I'm there, I can grab my bat! Let's see how far I can shove it down his throat until his jaw breaks.

"I'm going to gut him!" I slam my hand down on the table when I get lost in my fantasies, but Declan shoves the side of my arm to make me realize where we are again. Cain only chuckles as he waves to the nervous crowd with his fake grin to try and keep everyone calm. I apologize for my outburst with a nod, but my skin vibrates with the need to rip this guy apart.

"Let's take a walk. Maybe we can stop our target in the parking lot. I don't think Micah can wait much longer," Cain teases as he slaps my back and gets up from our table.

I stand abruptly, my combat boots already slamming to the ground towards the Christmas display in this awful, monstrous building. Declan grumbles under his breath as I charge towards our target without slowing. I don't know why they're so focused on us blending. No one will miss this guy.

When we get to the giant tree with Santa's chair, Cain curses under his breath when he sees our target. Sometimes, for people like us whose first memories are the deep rot of humanity, life gives us the ability to see evil in *monster's* eyes. People usually all look the same to me, only the wicked ones draw my attention.

And he's just like the rest of them. And like all the others that get in my way, his time is up. My grin pulls up as my muscles relax when I lock my eyes on our next target, sitting there laughing with families who are completely unaware of the vile intent behind his eyes. They don't have to worry after today though. We're here to take out the trash. Finally. It's been days since my hands have been bloody.

My instincts try to keep my glare on the target, but a tempting blur in the background pulls my focus. Within seconds, every detail of her becomes clearer until I'm aware of her completely. Her graceful movements, her command of the space around her, the awareness she holds from everyone. She blends perfectly in with the *people* around her, better than the three of us could ever imagine, but her eyes are as dark and tortured as ours.

Is she here to kill Santa too?

My nerves are in a trance as my feet move me to the side of the wide hallway away from the crowd so I can get a better look at her. She's wearing this elf costume that I would normally be irritated by. I mean, it sure seems like we all gloss over the fact that Santa has a slave army. But the way it pulls tight over her wide hips, how it dips around her full breasts…if elves look like this, I might change my mind about the concept of Father Christmas. Her wild, red curls

3

are barely contained by her hat as she bounces around doing three different jobs, as if she's putting on a show, just for me.

"What's wrong?" Declan stands in front of me wearing the same concern on his face that he always has right before I lose my mind and go dark. But all I see is light right now.

"Look at her." I grab his shoulders and turn him around, my eyes not being able to move away from her for a second. His brows shoot up as a low breath escapes him when he sees her, and as Cain follows our gaze, he reacts the same.

Maybe she's the one. Ever since the three of us were bonded in blood as kids, I always believed we were one member short. *Our Queen.*

"She's something else." Cain runs his hand through his hair to push it back as his heated gaze runs over her.

"It's more than that. She's…" I struggle to find the words, this ache in my chest stealing my senses as it reaches out for her. They've never believed that our missing limb existed. They didn't want to bring someone else down into our lives, but she's already here.

"Before you get away from yourself, she's just a woman. A civilian. Tell me you understand." Declan turns to address me again as he shoves my hand off his shoulders.

"No, she's not." I take a threatening step forward, violence surging through me at the thought of anyone keeping me from my little elf. "Look into her eyes. She's one of us."

When I shove him to turn around again, he listens, only because he doesn't want to make a scene. He knows I don't give a shit about that. I crave *people* shaking in their boots around me. I could introduce myself to her by slitting Santa's throat right fucking now.

Cain is still leaning against the wall, tilting his head as he observes her with a longing smirk. But it's not enough. How can they not see it?

Finally, her eyes land on the three of us staring at her. Her brows shoot up for a second before her cheeks explode with color. She quickly turns away and continues taking pictures of

4

Santa, but she showed the guys what I couldn't put into words. She already has my back. One look is all we needed.

As Cain stands tall and narrows his eyes, Declan observes her more carefully as well. I don't breathe yet, debating if I'm about to destroy everyone's day here at the mall and start shooting, or if the two of them will make the right decision.

"I'm not saying we're doing anything." Declan rolls his shoulders back as he clears his throat. "But I'll look into her."

"I'm not leaving her." My body moves closer to her, the pull she has on me already dominating me. The fact that either of them has hesitation only means we need to be closer to her. Her energy just affects me the most because I'm the strongest. They may disagree, but I'll show her I'm unbeatable.

When Declan shoves his hand against my chest to stop me, my rage takes over any restraint I have left. I slam my elbow against his jaw and reach around to get my knife, but both of them grab me as quick as they can and shove me through a door into a service hallway.

Knowing if I get an inch, they'll both end up with another wound, they work together to restrain my hands and slam me down on the concrete floor. I curse my threats at them, spooking someone down the hall as they shriek and slam a door closed.

"Just trust me! I need you to wait." Declan rams his knee into my back and pushes my head into the floor, but I don't stop fighting for a second. I snatch his arm and twist at the same time as he grabs my other arm to hold it onto my back, putting us in a race to see whose shoulder dislodges first.

"I bet she'd like it if you proved you were patient!" Cain calls up to me as I trap his neck and shoulder between my legs. "Show her how strong you are…idiot!" he gurgles out as I choke him.

When his words register past the violence drumming past my ears, I let my entire body go slack as my grin pulls up. They both roll off me and kick me to the other side of the hall while grumbling their annoyance and catching their breath.

She's going to see how powerful I am as I hold myself back. No one can do that. I'll show her.

Chapter Two

Aria

June

The clothing store I work at is short staffed today, of course, and it's our summer Hot Deals week, which means my feet are in hell.

I'm starting to feel like inspector gadget though; whipping my price gun out of my belt, clipping tags on new clothes, scanning more items in an hour than I usually see in a week, all while running around the store trying to tell the part-timers what to do. Like I said...feet hell.

When my co-worker goes on break, I get to stay behind the counter, feeling like I'm on a small break of my own now that no one's coming to check-out yet. For a smaller store, there's still a ton of people here, all cramming together to take advantage of our summer sales.

As I fold some clothes on the counter beside the register, I close my eyes and take a few deep breaths, absorbing the constant hum of conversations and arguments surrounding me. The perfect place to hide.

Everyone's voices blend together, but a certain tone stands out. Angry. Resentful. Cruel.

My eyes snap open as I whip my head in the direction of the gravelly voice, finding a middle aged, sweaty asshole reprimanding his daughter who's just trying to figure out which shirt she wants. They're on the other side of the store, tucked into a corner, but they're all I see.

"You're only getting one, you spoiled little bitch. Just like your mother. You have five seconds or we're fucking

7

leaving," he quietly sneers to her, making her shoulders tilt in even farther as she cringes away from him, visibly fearing he's going to hit her in public. But men like him wait until no one's watching.

My unblinking eyes never move from him as I leave the counter, my body instinctively pulling me towards her.

"Can I help?" I try using my sweet, customer service voice, but it comes out harsh and cutting as my furious glare stays locked on him. My own anger brews so viciously inside me that I have to force my hands into fists to hide that they're shaking.

"We're fine," he snaps out as he puts his hand up right in my face, but I don't back down an inch. I promised myself I never would again. "She just can't make a fucking decision. She barely fits in either of them, so it doesn't even matter." As he lowers his venomous tone and glares at his daughter, I picture ramming my price gun into his eye socket.

When I take a quick glance at the young girl that he feels he has the right to shame, I see the signs even clearer now…the long sleeves even though it's hot outside, the hair covering half her face, undoubtedly hiding a bruise underneath, the way she holds herself to be as small as possible, desperately trying not to anger him.

"Are you too stupid to know that children grow?" I don't hide a single ounce of condescension in my tone as I take a small sidestep to urge the girl behind me.

"Excuse me…cunt?" The pig's face turns red in seconds as he stands tall to try intimidating me. "Why don't you thank her? Because you're not getting anything for your birthday now." He gestures from his daughter to me, but he made the mistake of grazing my arm. That's all I needed.

Using my loudest, shocked gasp, I throw myself over to the side, landing loudly on the shelves of t-shirts beside me. Everyone gasps and takes in the scene I'm creating as I whip my fake, hurt, terrified face to him and grab my arm before wincing in pain to make a good show.

"What the fuck are you doing?" He takes a step towards me, but I scramble away, putting my hand up as if he's about to punch me. A few people around us grumble and move out of the way or shift forward to help me, making him realize everyone's watching.

Holding down my satisfied grin, I rush behind the desk to grab the phone, knowing I need to hurry before he bolts. I quickly call security as the *pig* backs up to his daughter, grabbing her arm in a bruising grip, which makes me feel beyond guilty, but hopefully I can get some revenge for her today.

I would have loved to watch someone as immense as my uncle lay into him when I was a kid, just once.

"*Security,*" the guard on the phone answers.

"Hi, this is store number 3417. One of my customers is belligerent. He called me a cunt and hit me!" I rush out, making sure my voice is loud enough for everyone to hear as the pig drags his daughter out of here, every single eye in the store on them. Someone at least needs to slow him down! Shit. "He's wearing a blue polo and dark jeans, and..."

"*Don't worry. Micah's around the corner,*" the guard on the phone cuts me off, the collected, assured glint in his voice calming me down a fraction. I take a deep breath, trying not to lose sight of the pig through the crowd.

"He's getting away." I go up on my toes to see over the people in my way, spotting him still yanking his daughter along by her arm. "He's almost at the..."

My words get caught in my throat when Micah glides in front of the pig, right at the exit. I'm not sure if it's just in my head, but everyone seems to hold their breath. This is usually the uneasy reaction Micah gets.

I haven't really talked to him yet, but I'm delighted that he's the one who showed up. Some of the weirdest guys are hired to work security here at the mall, and they usually let their little power go straight to their heads. But the three guys that were hired earlier this year don't need a taser to keep customers in line. They just radiate this *authority* that's hard to disagree with.

They've broken up fights and chased down thieves without breaking a sweat. It's been thrilling to watch and gossip about. They're off-kilter a bit, but it helps that they're also gorgeous, tall, tattooed, and oddly polite.

"Is he there?" the other guard on the phone asks, his voice continuing to ease my nerves.

"Yeah, he's…" I struggle to speak as I watch Micah take a step forward, the severe energy he exudes making everyone seem to take a step back. He's so…unique.

Gripping the phone tightly in my hand, my eyes refuse to move off Micah as the pig releases his daughter who scurries off to the side.

"Listen…I didn't do shit. Okay?" the pig tries to explain as he puts his hands up, his voice booming over the unnerving silence.

Micah puts his finger up to his lips to shush him as he takes another step closer. Slowly, he tilts his head, making his snow-white hair fall to the side, his wide blue eyes slicing through the decreasing space between him and the pig.

I'm oddly frustrated when Micah starts whispering, wishing I could interject and give my fake story. I take a step closer, intending on going over there to really sell the abuse I suffered.

"Stay behind the counter."

I flinch when the guy on the phone gives me a demand, having forgotten I was even speaking to him.

"Don't I need to explain what happened?" I ask as I lean against the ledge, still watching the odd interaction Micah is having with the pig.

"You don't have to worry about that. We'll take care of it." The man calms me again.

"Thanks…I'm Aria, by the way. And you're…"

"Declan."

"Oh, you're another one of the new security guys?" My smile pulls wide as I put on a slightly friendlier tone, never having had a full conversation with any of them before. Jenna tried to invite Cain to lunch since he seems like the least hostile of them, but he respectfully declined. Declan doesn't really speak to anyone as far as I've seen.

"That I am. Now tell me, what's Micah doing?"

"I'm not sure. He just put his hand on the p...the *man's* shoulder, and it looks like he's…" I tilt over the counter a bit to try seeing the pig's face to gauge what kind of conversation they're having, but his back is still to me. "He's just talking to him."

"Hopefully, he's teaching him a lesson. He clearly doesn't know how to be a man yet, right?" Declan's raspy voice transforms from soothing me to heating my skin as he unstiffens his tone.

"He's not a man. He's a piece of filth." I keep my voice quiet enough that the people around can't hear me, but I have a hunch that Declan has a dark sense of humor like I do.

"If I had my way, we'd just drop him off the bridge," he lets out an amused breath, and I join him as a giggle rises in my throat.

"That's a good idea. He'd have a few seconds to think about how he wasted his life." My fingers twirl a piece of my hair on their own accord as warmth spreads to my cheeks, but I stand straight and remind myself to act like I'm scared and hurt, not flirting about killing someone.

"How would you do it?" Declan's voice hardens a bit, losing his playful glint, not helping the heat in my face.

"How would I…"

"If there were no repercussions, and you got to punish that man…how would you do it?"

"I…" I go to lie and say jail or something, but when the pig turns around out of Micah's grip, my words get lodged in my throat as I see his face, beat red, tears streaming over his cheeks, his eyes filled with…fear. It's so rare to see repulsive people like him afraid. I need to know what Micah said to him.

Micah's eyes never move from the pig as he sheepishly gestures for his daughter to leave with him. He keeps his head down and his tail tucked between his legs as he darts out of here, never making a move to touch or hurry his daughter. The level of satisfaction rolling through me at seeing that man broken down from a few words is a bit shameful. I shouldn't want that so badly. I thought my thirst for revenge was sated.

"I'd trap him alone. Drag the suffering out as long as I could. Make sure he died knowing no one was going to save him." The truth of what I did tumbles out of me before I can stop it. As I realize my creepy overshare was out loud, I take in a quick gasp and try figuring out a way to talk myself out of it, but Declan's chuckling stops me.

"That's far better than the bridge. I'll make sure to come to you next time someone steps out of line."

I can't help but chuckle in relief, but it becomes a bit forced when Micah locks eyes with me. His grin pulls up gradually, kind of disturbing like the grinch's. He gives me a wink before spinning around and strolling down the hallway, leaving a contrastingly eerie yet excited impression on me as I feel the need to run after him and beg him to tell me what he said. I barely hold back from doing just that as the customers in the store go back to shopping now that there's no more drama.

"Thank you for staying on the phone. And please thank Micah."

"I will. Are you alright though?"

"Oh…" I suddenly remember that I told them I was hit. "It wasn't so bad."

"I'm glad."

As customers start moving towards the register, I know I need to hang up, but something about Declan's tone makes it seem like he's in no rush to do so. I wouldn't mind talking to him either, but…

"I should get back to work."

"Right…call if you need anything, Aria."

"I will." I bounce a bit on my heels as that giddy sensation spreads over my skin again. His voice is sexy as fuck.

"See you soon." With that, he hangs up, leaving warmth on my face, probably for the rest of the day.

That was unusual, but it turned out better than I thought. Hopefully, whatever Micah said disturbed the pig enough for him to leave his daughter alone for…forever. I guess I can't control that. In my mind though, he's being thrown off a bridge as we speak.

That's the thought that has me smiling the rest of the day.

Shelby Manuel

Chapter Three
Aria

Six months later

On the lighter side of Christmas, people are popping anti-anxiety meds to deal with their dreadful families that they *love*, but that also makes you feel like shit the entire time. And then on the other side of the holidays, the majority of people in this country are more worried about an insane increase of violence, self-harm, car accidents, and assaults.

I don't think it matters where you fall on that spectrum, most of us choose to lie to ourselves about it being a horrible time of year. It all seems smoothed over with expensive twinkling lights, an abundance of food that'll give you heartburn, forced generosity, and gifts that most people return. But it's *magical.*

I've been working in malls since I was fourteen, and it doesn't matter how people feel about Christmas, they generally end up here at some point. Watching them all failing to cope with the stress of the holidays while desperately trying to revel in the atmosphere is a sick fascination and annual tradition of mine. I've never seen people lie to themselves more or grit their teeth through it together.

The energy shifts when the first decorations go up. Most of the people who work here start sweating, knowing the most hectic days are ahead of us, filled with entitlement and screaming children. To me, it's hilarious.

That's why every year, no matter what mall I'm working at, I always volunteer to be right in the thick of the misery. Right in the action of every dad sweating as they try to wrangle in children and carry the bags, and mothers trying to make sure everyone smiles while just wanting to punch someone in the head.

Every year, I work with Santa and take pictures of kids having an awkward as hell time. Most children are afraid while their parents shove them at some random man until I can get the perfect shot. I bet they'd be a lot more hesitant if they knew most of the Santa's are random old dudes who have a flask hidden in their pocket.

Usually, I dress as an elf, but this year I have the 'honor' of being Mrs. Claus. That's what my boss, Randy, called it at least. But when he started rambling just to hear his own voice, he admitted that I was too busty to be an elf. He then went on and on about my figure while constantly glancing at my breasts. *Charming.*

I'm actually excited not to be in those tight leggings. And this gives me some more real-world experience to try out my makeup skills. I've been moving from city to city for most of my life, meeting amazing people, and then going to the next. I've learned a few random skills along the way. One of my roommates did special effects in L.A, and she taught me a bunch of things. I love showing off my talents.

"Aria!" my coworker, Jenna, shouts from our store as I get closer. I stop to talk to her and help her fold some new stock, but a family rushing around me bumps right into my shoulder. After scowling at them, I weave my way through the already crowded hallway to get over to Jenna.

"Holy crap, it's only ten in the morning," I chuckle as I slip into the store and hoist my duffle bag over my shoulder.

"What's all that?" She jerks her chin at my heavy bag as she turns to the table to fold some shirts.

"It's my work out clothes, and…*my new identity.*" I fake the sweet, old lady voice I've been trying out for Mrs. Claus, getting Jenna to bark out a laugh.

"I totally forgot. I've been trying to block this holiday out of my head. And that I'll be working *in* this shithole without you." She glances at me with a dramatic sneer. "I'm so glad

16

I'm dating Eric. He doesn't celebrate Christmas, and it's so much less stressful at his house. They're on the far better track than mine," she rants easily as she throws some t-shirts over for me to fold. After dropping my bag to the floor as my hand starts going numb, I roll my shoulders back and start helping her fold some clothes.

"There's no blocking out the shitshow here. Are the three of us still on for dinner and drinks on Saturday? I know it's nuts with all the traffic in town lately, but I need to get out," I grumble as a few people come into the store.

"Hell yes. My brother and his family are in town and staying at our mom's. I'm still in her basement, unfortunately, so she expects me up there at every free second, but my nephews are little assholes. I miss when they were cute and loved me." She stops to let the new customers know about the sale we have going on and the new stock near the side.

"Can I stay at your place after? And maybe this whole week? Unless you'll have *company*." She suggestively wags her eyebrows as she bumps my shoulder.

"My couch is your couch, as always. And I can't even remember the last time I had company other than you," I snort back a laugh as I shake my head.

"This is my favorite time for some temporary mistle-toeing. Maybe you and Santa can *bake some cookies* this year." She twirls the pair of underwear that she was folding as she gives me a teasing grin.

"Kurt?" I fake a theatrical gag as I use the table to steady myself. "He's a sixty-year-old man who only talks about rugby. I'll take a pass on *Santa* this year." I shiver at the mention of Kurt. He's the regular Santa around here, I guess. I met him last year when I was his elf, and he almost made me back out for this year. I've been creeped out by a few Santa's, but he took the cake.

"Oh, you didn't hear?" Jenna lowers her voice as she turns to me, her move for when she's about to spill some tea. I drop the shorts I was folding to turn to her as well. "Last year, he just dropped off the map. His mother put out a missing person report, but there's been no trace other than his costume was found a few weeks after in some ditch outside of town…covered in blood." She mimes an explosion with her hands as she steps back.

"Oh my God! How have I not heard about that?" I slap my hand over my mouth when a laugh erupts out of me, making Jenna stifle her giggle as she hits my arm.

"Because you know I hate talking about gory shit, and in the two years I've known you, I'm still the only bitch you like talking to." She gives a customer a fake smile before leaning back to continue talking quietly. "I guess when Randy asked for someone to replace Kurt, only one person signed up, and Kelly told me he's not bad to look at…so maybe this year, Santa can show you his *chimney*." She elbows me with a big grin, and I throw my head back with a laugh, only to get glared at by some of the customers around us, probably pissed that we're not working.

"That's my cue." Jenna straightens out her clothes and plasters on her smile. "See you later." She slaps my ass and spins around to help some of them as I lug my bag back over my shoulder.

The probable murder of Kurt should be sticking around in my mind as I walk towards the giant Christmas display where Santa's chair is, but what's really bugging me is what Jenna said about knowing me for two years. Have I really been here that long? I didn't even realize.

This city isn't different or special compared to where I've lived before, but that drive inside me to keep moving and hiding hasn't really been affecting me lately. I don't think anyone is looking for me anymore, but I'm always careful to stay a nomad. But I thought about getting a cat last month. Two years is a long time for me to stay anywhere.

When I get to the Christmas display in the middle of the mall, I take a second to see how truly massive it got over the past week. The chair is more like a red loveseat, wrapped in ribbon, but above it towers the giant white tree in the middle that rises almost three stories of this excessively massive mall. There's a red and green fence all around the display, herding the families around the front to line up for hours just to take a picture with some guy.

We don't open for another hour, but there's already people lined up. Now the show can begin.

As I hold down my sadistic smirk at the miserable people forcing themselves to seem happy, I walk around to the back of the display to the little shed hidden within the tree where we change and get ready. I can't help but roll my eyes when I spot Randy standing in front of the shed, texting on his phone, his too-tight suit pulling across his protruding belly as he scowls at whatever he's reading.

"Good, you're finally here. No elves today, so all you have is Santa. You heard about Kurt, right?" he monotones without looking up from his phone.

"It's opening day for this though. That's a lot to expect of…" I start telling him the craziness that he's actually asking of me.

"You'll do great. Cain will help you." He jerks his chin behind me, still looking down at his phone. At the mention of his name, I take in a quick breath as my brows shoot up. No way I'm that lucky.

"Cain? One of the security guys?" I ask as I try to hold down my hopeful excitement. It'll be worth the sore feet if this is real.

"I have to say, this outfit looks way better than my mall cop get-up." Cain strolls around me holding his Santa suit in a black bag. His dark brown, wavy hair is pushed back over his ears, his sharp, stubble covered jaw line looks like blades, and his wide lips pull up at the sides as his piercing green eyes lock onto mine. *Wow.* He's even more handsome up close.

Randy rambles for a moment, finally looking up from his phone, but he's just gibberish to me now. Cain and his buddies still unfortunately don't socialize much, but they've been asked out by plenty of people who work here, and a few customers. If the gossip I've heard is true, they always graciously refuse, so even though the three of them have caught my eye as well, I never took my shot. Fantasies are far better than rejection.

But now, I'll actually be working with one of them! It takes everything in me not to giggle in delight like I'm a teenager again.

"It gets hot in these outfits though…so most Santa's go down to their boxers." The words escape my mouth before I have the chance to run them over in my head. Cain's dark brows rise as his grin grows, burning embarrassment into my skin.

"You don't mind helping?" He gestures his head to the shed door beside us.

"With your boxers?" My eyes fly open as I glance at both men, but Randy frowns back in confusion.

"What? I was telling him you were going to do your own makeup. And fix your…hair." Randy gestures vaguely to my curly red hair like it's some animal. "Help him too. Santa doesn't have face tattoos." He points to both of us, scolding us like children. Without another word, he storms off and calls someone on the phone as I glare after him.

"Does he ever shut up?" Cain mumbles under his breath, and I pull my bottom lip into my mouth as I try not to blush, but it's useless.

"I distract myself by trying to figure out what food made the stain on his shirt when he's rambling." I shake my head as I hurry into the shed, suddenly being presented with more work than I think we have time for now. As I dump my bag on the ground, I almost laugh when I realize how mad everyone will be if we're late.

"You tune him out? I thought maybe you were just horrified I was going to strip down," he chuckles low in his throat as he comes in after me, having to duck his head a bit since he's so tall. He shakes off his leather jacket before plopping down on the stool and leaning his hands on his legs, relaxing as if he's not in a rush. "Maybe not a great first impression?" He shrugs as he gives me another delicious smirk and stretches his long limbs in the cabin, filling the space.

The sporadic, dark tattoos that go from his fingers up his arm, leading to his chest that's covered by his white t-shirt

20

pulls my focus completely, but I shake my head to stay focused. He smells so good though. Shit.

"Actually…my first impression of you happened when I was in the food court, last May. A few of my coworkers and I watched you sarcastically applaud some guy who dropped his garbage near the can until he picked it up. Quite impressive. But…I'm Aria." When I hold out my hand, he stands again, making me back up a step until my ass hits the table, but he doesn't step back or sit down, instead closing the distance.

"I *saw* you before that." He slides his hand into mine as he steps into the fiery air around me, forcing me to pull my bottom lip into my mouth again. Is this normal? Is he mad? "That big, empty department store was throwing an easter egg hunt."

At his words, I finally let out my breath with a shaking chuckle, "Yeah, we all dressed up. It was so weird, but I kind of loved it. I was working the ticket booth." I drop my gaze to the floor when he won't look away.

"You were dressed as a feral bunny." The corner of his lips twitch into a smirk as he glances down at our hands, bringing my realization to the fact that he's still holding mine. "I'm curious to see if Mrs. Claus is a cuter version, but I liked the bunny. Sweet and deadly." Instead of shaking my hand, he slides his thumb across my palm, the small move catching the words in my throat. *Be cool!*

"I got in trouble for that costume actually." I slip out of his grasp to busy myself with taking my jacket off, needing to get out of this moment or I'll start sweating. "I thought it was clever, 'Rabid Rabbit', but I made some kid cry, and his mom complained." When my hands won't stop trembling, I tighten them into a fist as I turn around, my heart beating faster from just social interaction. I need to get out more.

"I thought you looked great. The blood dripping off your fangs was…perfect," he murmurs from right behind me, continuing to somehow be more socially awkward than me. "Now…" He snaps out of his oddly intimate introduction as he spins around me to lean against the table and clasp his hands in his lap. "It's a shame I can't have any blood on my teeth, but I can't wait to see what I'm going to look like in about forty years. Work your magic." He gives me a charming grin, letting us officially come out of the intense energy he trapped me in. *Sweet and deadly.*

"I think that's the best compliment I've ever gotten," I admit begrudgingly under my breath as I grab my makeup bag and stand in front of him.

"I guess I'll have to work harder," he says smoothly as he spreads his knees, prompting me to stand between them to do his makeup. Is he flirting with me? Maybe he's joking or bored or something.

Swallowing my nerves and trying to push away my self-conscious-asshole part of my brain, I step in between his knees, the sides of my thighs brushing against his jeans. My skin surges with energy from the intensity of his gaze as I take out some concealer and color corrector. After mixing some on my hand, I dampen a new sponge and start working on his face.

For a moment too long, no words are spoken, but I don't know how to fix it. I discreetly wipe a stray bead of sweat from my forehead, but I feel like I'm expanding, becoming more aware of every movement of my plump body. I'm the one taking up all the space. Next time, we're doing this in the break room.

I just pretend to be hyper focused on what I'm doing instead of showing him how much I feel like I have to rip off my skin. The vines that wrap in front of his ear are the first ink I cover. It would be easier if he turned his head, but he keeps his emerald eyes on me the entire time. He closes them when I brush my thumb across his cheek to blend out some of the concealer. Jenna is never going to believe me when I tell her this happened.

"How old are you?" Again, the words rush out of my mouth before my brain can stop them.

When his eyes open, his lips pull back into a teasing smirk. "Thirty. You?"

I almost breathe out a sigh of relief, fearing for a moment that he was fresh out of college or something. I'd feel icky thinking he was hot. His face is deceiving, looking like he's been through so much but retained a level of boyish curiosity. "I'm twenty-six. Have you always been a mall cop?" When I realize how he might take that, I stop dabbing his chin with a gasp. "I didn't mean any offence. I swear. It's…I was just curious, not…" I stammer as I back up, but his hand wraps around my wrist to stop me before I see him moving.

"No offence taken, Brat," he teases me with a sideways grin before shrugging and leaning back on his hand, stretching his legs out farther to almost tap his feet against the other side of the shed, trapping me. I shake my head at myself, forcing my lips to smile and continue working, thinking far too much for a simple conversation. "This mall ain't so bad. It's a sweet side gig where I eat like a king and hang out with my partners, threatening pricks for fun. And where I get to finally meet Mrs. Claus." I swear his cheeks turn red before I can dab blush on them.

"That's a more positive outlook than most people have when describing any job they do. You could be on the mall's recruitment ads," I gibe to cover my awkwardness as I go back to adding a few shaded lines on his tanned face, glad to have not offended him. I'm terrible at flirting, but I don't think insulting him is a good start. "Your…partners? Like…" I try to find a way to figure out if he means boyfriends or business. Maybe both? They do seem really close.

"The three of us grew up together like brothers. We own our own business. That's my main job. But this one has infinitely more perks." He slides his tongue out to wet his lips before I can add a bit of glue to his jaw for the beard.

"Neat! What do you guys do?" My brows raise with my curiosity. I knew they'd be interesting.

"We're freelancers…" Tilting his head, his smile turns warm and lazy like he's in no rush to leave this shed, but as his eyes narrow, he hesitates to continue for a moment longer than normal. "We do a lot of home destruction." The muscles along his cheek tighten as he tries to hold down a smirk. Maybe he's lying, or he could possibly be embarrassed.

"I bet that's such a rage relief, just…" As I mime taking a bat and smashing the wall of the cabin, he tosses his head back with a throaty chuckle, but I quickly shush him, knowing we're minutes away from the door being knocked on because we're taking too long.

"Careful, I might start recruiting you." He mimes straightening a tie. "You like working here?" He helps me put on his beard, but I jolt when his knuckles brush mine, not wanting him to trap me again. I quickly place it along his sharp jaw up to his ears before stepping back, wanting more of his intense energy, but I'm far too overstimulated in this moment.

"Most people hate it, but I've always kind of liked it. It's sometimes fun to be front row for the slow collapse of capitalism; *the mall.*" I dramatically gesture around us with a small chuckle as his amused gaze leisurely trails over my face. I probably shouldn't be this turned on at work, but even though this was odd, it was way better than my flirting usually goes.

"Doesn't sound like a place where you could add many names to your nice list." He fakes a deep, rolling Santa voice as he furrows his brows with worry, truly looking like a concerned Saint Nick. I did great.

"You're the one who makes the list, *Santa.*" I use my old lady voice as I spin to the mirror to finish up my own makeup. We can both see my face turning red when he steps behind me, his body close enough to radiate heat into me.

"I'm a new man," he says quietly before glancing down at me as I smile at my handy work. "If I have to make the list, should I start with you? Nice…or naughty?" He wraps his finger around one of my curls behind me as his gaze snaps back up to meet mine in the reflection.

I almost roll my eyes at the cheesy line, but out of his lips, it feels *scalding.* Steeling my nerves, I finish up the blush on my nose before turning around to face him, being much closer than I was prepared for.

Looking up at him through my lashes, I try desperately not to laugh as I murmur, "I guess you'll let me know on Christmas."

Chapter Four
Cain

A few weeks later

One hard knock on the cabin door lets me know Declan is here. "Give me a sec," I call out as I pull off the horrible, scratchy suit and slip on my normal clothes. Ripping the beard off, I wince when the glue takes out a few strands of my actual hair, but my jaw needs a second to stretch. Grabbing one of the makeup wipes that Aria left me, I aggressively clean off the old man makeup.

She stays in costume during her break, but when I do, no one leaves me alone to eat, and they're unaware of how much Santa would like to jam a fork into their throat. And this way, Aria has to redo my makeup, so I'll take any excuse to have her hands back on me. She doesn't seem to mind either.

After throwing on a hoody, I stroll out to find Declan glaring at Aria as she rambles uncomfortably about what movie she watched last night while she fidgets with her fingers. She's still wary around him, but he just does nothing to help himself. She'll learn soon that his mask to hide what's inside isn't as good as hers or mine.

"Ready for lunch, *my love?*" I gently touch her back, using the same name for her that I use when I'm Santa, which always makes her curling smile pull up her plump lips. She gives me a nod before leading the way to the food court, her dress swaying as she struts ahead of us.

"Did you have to text Micah so fucking early that we were doing this?" Declan grumbles quietly as we trail Aria. "He's been useless all day. Almost gave a shoplifter a concussion." He's drowned out by Aria's story and the crowd of shoppers around us, but instead of responding, I just shrug as I stifle my laugh. I've loved not working security lately. I have a much better job now, even though everyone except her makes me want to rip out my gun.

This morning, when I found out Jenna had the day off and Aria would be eating lunch alone, I figured I'd give the guys another chance to get a little closer to her. Jenna, like most people, is not a big fan of us, mostly Micah. He tries to act like everyone else when he has to, but he simply doesn't believe he *should* have to. If he's around someone long enough, he tells them what he's really thinking. Which is often unnerving.

I sent them the text that Aria agreed to have lunch with us as soon as she told me. I bet Micah's been driving Declan crazy. We're all going a bit mad though. That reminds me…

"Everything's set up for next week, right?" I ask Declan quietly as I smile at Aria when she glances back at us to see if we're still behind her. We're always behind her.

"Everything's good. We'll be the only staff until the next morning. But we'll be long gone by then." Declan's stern face softens for a moment when she looks at him and swallows down her nerves.

I've only ever seen him do three things for himself in the twenty-five years we've known each other. The first was slicing his father's throat to save his own life, and the second was years later when he stole an engraved switchblade from a pawn shop. The name was faded, but we could see a clear 'D' on it. He thought it was fate. He's had that knife ever since.

The third thing he's ever done for himself was agreeing to let us stay here and investigate her. I took me a couple months to truly understand what Micah was trying to show us. Aria is gorgeously tempting, and I would have jumped at the chance to have a taste, but we don't invite anyone into our lives or spend time with another person for more than a few hours.

It didn't take me long to realize she was different though. Beyond all that we've learned about her, it's so clear that she doesn't belong in this community of 'upstanding' citizens.

There's a much darker society we know she'll thrive in, and she'll hopefully be with us. Micah was right. That fucking maniac took three seconds to realize it.

I'm typically liberal and experimental with the few hours I show to the random women in the equally as random cities we work in, but I've barely been able to look at anyone else for a year. My hand is getting sore.

I feared Declan would never truly see her, and it would cause a rift. I'd like to think the bond between the three of us is unbreakable, but if he decided that we had to leave Aria alone, I don't know if I could. And I have no doubt that we'd be making a mortal enemy out of Micah.

We may have more enemies than the average person, but none as dangerously unpredictable as that crazy bastard. We'd never be able to close our eyes again. The fact that he's spent the last year somehow losing his mind with rage that he can't take her, but also following the rules that we've laid out for him to keep his distance, is the closest thing to a miracle I've ever seen.

When Aria sees him sitting at the table ahead of us in the busy food court, no one daring to sit near him, his wide eyes staring right at her, her steps blamelessly falter. She's right to be cautious, but she's being pulled closer to each of us every day. She just doesn't realize it yet.

Micah stands when we approach, his black security outfit seeming to get tighter as he flexes each of his svelte muscles. His snow-white hair is tamer than it usually is, but he still looks like a young, fit, mad scientist who's covered in sporadic ink. His lips menacingly lift on the side as his eyes track her, not helping to diminish the threatening aura he's giving off.

"Hey." Aria gives him a small wave as she glances back at me again for direction on how to proceed, probably misreading his severe energy as enraged. She'll realize soon that she's the only one he looks at like that.

"I got you food." Micah points to her tray on the table.

"Oh…wow, thank you. I love Pad Thai. You didn't have to do that. How did you know it was my favorite?" she chuckles lightly as she sits down and tucks the bottom of her dress beside her.

"He told me." He jerks his chin at me without taking his eyes off her.

"You were talking about it last week. We like it too." I drop down beside her and throw an arm over the back of her chair so I can see her cheeks flush again.

I always feel like I'm showing her off to my guys, which makes an animalistic side of me pound on my chest. That side of me would love to think I'm the only man she needs, but I know it'll take all three of us. For the past few weeks though, I've gotten to sadistically watch the two of them struggle as she gets close to me *first*. Micah's been taking it out on me by waking me up with a bucket of ice every morning. It's worth it.

As she gives me an appreciative smile, it takes everything in me not to grab her and slam my lips against hers. Soon.

"How's being Mrs. Claus today?" Micah leans his elbows on the table as his gaze continues to devour her. "Did you yell at any annoying parents? Did you get to use the tripping tactic I showed you? With all those big ass bags and your puffy dress, they'll never see your foot." He darts his eyes from her to her food, wondering why she isn't eating yet, despite firing questions at her. I widen my eyes to hint that he should slow down, but his are still boring a hole through her.

She can't hold his forceful stare, but I don't interfere like Declan instructed. She needs to get used to us all quickly, much faster than she's prepared for in my opinion. She's still going to be terrified.

"I haven't had to, yet. They're all being oddly polite this year. I think they're all too afraid of Cain." She brings her shoulders up as she grins again and takes a bite of food, her cheeks continuing to flush.

Micah's lips twist in anger as he slips his hands under the table, probably to stop himself from slamming a fist into me. I'm not sure if he's experienced jealousy before between the three of us, but he's managing better than I thought. Declan sips his coffee while scanning the people around us, but I can tell he's still aware of every movement she makes. We all are.

"Would you like some?" Aria asks Micah softly as she slides her tray across the table to him. All his tensed muscles relax as his brows pull together when he realizes she noticed he was upset. She might not know that the reason he's mad is that he'd rather she was fighting people with his skills rather than relying on me for protection, but she can still tell something is bothering him.

"I'm okay. I'm just glad to feed you." He leans his elbows back on the table, and I turn my head to stifle my laugh as Declan shakes his head with a scowl. That's definitely not a normal thing to say to a person who he's only spoken to a handful of times, but she handles it pretty well.

She lets out a small giggle as she pinches her brows in confusion, her blush spreading down her neck. Micah seems unfazed, and completely forgets we're surrounded by people when Aria picks up her story of the horror movie she watched last night. As she eats her food and rambles away, all three of us get our fill of her while we can. The amount of restraint we've shown should be rewarded, but she won't see it that way. Yet.

Growing up, Christmas was a time that my mother struggled harder with money and her addiction, which meant life for me turned into a more excruciating level of hell. After Declan took out his father, he came to help us, knowing what needed to be done for us to escape the life we were destined for.

Before the holidays were over, all the people who should have been protecting the three of us were annihilated. Our community was covered in blood, but we were free. We were three, scrawny, beaten kids that were dealt a life of pain from the minute we could breathe, but we had each other. Aria only had herself.

But this year, Christmas means something bigger than I've ever let myself imagine. The three of us will be getting the greatest gift there is.

And Aria will never be alone again.

Chapter Five

Aria

Christmas Eve

Usually, my fascination with Christmas dwindles down to exhaustion the closer we get to it, tapering off on Christmas eve. Everyone here is exhausted, and their patience is gone, but today, I swear I have a spring in my step.

The last few weeks have been so exciting, and the Christmas pictures have run smoother than ever. While there have been a few impatient parents, Cain's energy is just so delectably *intimidating*, that they don't argue much. Even in his Santa suit with the big beard on, all he has to do sometimes is stand up and tell the parents to calm down before they start apologizing.

As Mrs. Claus, I mostly keep people in line, hand out candy, and join in the picture if the parents want. It's tedious and loud, but Cain and I get to spend all day together. And it gets more fiery every day.

From the time I put his makeup on until he walks me to the bus at night, his eyes are on me. And every once in a while, he'll set me on his knee when we take pictures, which seems to stick with me all day.

He and I have been doing this little back and forth for weeks, but today, I'm making a big step and finally asking him out. I'm not one for making the first move, mostly because I lose my nerve, but I can't wait another day for him. I got him a gift, and I'm going to ask him out when I give it to him. I just need to do it as soon as I see him or I'll chicken out.

That's why when I pass by Jenna, we only wave to each other instead of my usual routine of stopping and helping her for a bit. She gives me a wink and a thumbs up for encouragement, having been the one I prepared my little speech on last week.

I thought all I wanted from him was, what I'm assuming would be a memorable, sweaty night. I don't get into relationships. I don't want to hurt them when I leave. But the more time I spend with him, I just want *more*. I'm not sure what it is exactly, but I'm also ready for a sweaty night to remember. I swear, he's been teasing me for weeks. My vibrator hasn't seen this much action in years.

For the first time in a while, I don't have to fake my smile as I hurry to the Christmas display. After dumping my bag off inside the shed, I rush to the loading bay, knowing that's where he hangs out before we start.

Walking through the mounds of stock in the back of the mall, I weave in and around the staff as I tuck my sweater tighter around myself. I'd hate to work back here in the cold, but they seem to like it. I only came to see Cain here once, but I felt like a creep because I had to ask three different people if they'd seen him. I'm trying to stay on the cute side of thirsty, but I know I'm making it obvious.

After I get to the side of the metal shelving, I tighten my sweater around myself even more and tuck my fingers in before shoving my shoulder into the door to get outside. A blast of cold hits me, reminding me how dumb I was for not wearing my coat as well. I was trying to look cute in my baggy, red sweater. Damnit.

"Hello, my love." Cain greets me with his Santa voice as he slides his jacket off, wasting no time before wrapping it around my shoulders. He doesn't look chilly at all as he's left in his black, long-sleeved shirt and dark jeans, reminding me how incredibly firm his body is.

I usually see him in a big Santa suit, so I always get a bit intimidated when I see him like this. I don't think leagues exist, as I'm attracted to people's energy…but he'd be way out of mine. As he lights up a smoke, I make sure to smile my greeting to Micah and Declan who are out with Cain.

34

"Hey guys. Thanks for the jacket. Sorry to interrupt…I just…" I abruptly realize I have no good excuse to come out here. Why didn't I think of one? Scrambling my brain for anything, I blurt out, "I was wondering if I could have a smoke? The holidays are finally getting to me." I bring my shoulders up as I twist my lips before shaking my head to get rid of the hair in my face.

"It finally broke you! I've never seen someone hold out for longer. I'm impressed," Micah says with an amused laugh as his smirk pulls to the side. His unique white hair flows smoothly to the back of his head, but always seems a little rough like he's just woken up. Besides that, and the thorned tattoo around his neck, I think it's his blue eyes that creep people out. There's an unflinching, penetrating quality about them that has earned him the nickname 'maniac,' which I think is equally cruel and adorably accurate. Even if it's a bit difficult to make conversation with him, he's sweet and hot in a Spike from Buffy kind of way.

"I'm just admitting the awfulness of it all is a worthy opponent. I will never break. Christmas is still the most sadistically entertaining time of the year," I snort back a giggle as Cain and Micah let out rolling laughs, their wide shoulders shaking in unison.

"What's your least favorite part?" Declan makes me flinch when he moves in close and lights up a smoke. He's the only one of the three that makes my skin crawl a little bit.

I don't think I've really had a full conversation with him in person yet. His short dark hair never moves like nothing on his body knows how to relax. He's also shaved the sides, revealing a dark pattern on his skin like he got tattoos of small blades cutting into him. He has the most ink that's visible, and it swirls up to his jaw that's somehow sharper than Cain's is. And he's a bit taller than the other two, but they all seem like giants to me. I'm not short at 5'8, but they tower over everyone.

"Of the holidays?" My brows pull in when I realize I haven't responded. He narrows his eyes and takes a long pull

35

of his smoke before flipping it around to me, reminding me what I'd asked them for. Is this weird? Sharing a smoke?

I glance behind him where Cain is leaning against the wall in a quiet conversation with Micah, leaving me alone with Declan and his smoke. I take it without a word, not willing to seem like I don't belong here.

"Yeah…when does it break you?" He stands directly in front of me and lights his own smoke, blocking me completely from the other two. This is a bit strange…but so was Cain when I first met him I guess.

"Tomorrow usually hits me." I bring my shoulders up. "I like the buildup to the big day the most." I raise my hand that's holding the smoke, hoping he doesn't expect me to inhale it. If I'm trying to seem cool, smoking will kill that when I roll over coughing. My lungs are weak as hell. "For at least a month, people let their excitement cloud more and more of the shit that's going on around them, only to come crashing down on the actual day when they realize it's just another Monday. I guess that kind of breaks me. But at least people like us get to finally relax." I cross my arms over myself, keeping the smoke between my fingers so it just burns out eventually. His wide lips pull up in the corners as his dark grey eyes search my face.

"Anticipation does seem to be the best part. Waiting for that one thing you can't live without." He clenches his fist in front of him, crushing his smoke and making me take in a quick breath as I urge my body not to back up. "Tomorrow will pass and come again, but if you could hold onto that feeling…if you got to keep that high you have right before the fall…would you?" As he takes a step closer, my brain scrambles for a moment.

I've asked myself over the last few weeks if Cain was just messing with me. If all the flirting he was doing was simply to pass the time. But maybe I've been reading him all wrong.

I haven't pried into how the three of them grew up, mostly because Cain gets this blank stare on his face any time I ask. They grew up like 'brothers' though, so I'm assuming foster care or something even rougher. But maybe whatever happened to them just made them all this intense, and no one has been flirting with me. Damn.

That thought brings my shoulders down a bit as reality comes crushing into me. It's probably better this way. I was getting far too into Cain, and I don't want to hurt when I leave. These have been a nice couple of weeks though.

"Would I keep the feeling you get right before the let down?" I clarify Declan's question as I drop the smoke to the ground, hoping he won't notice. Slowly, he nods as he presses his black boot against the smoke, moving another step closer and never taking his eyes off me. "No. There's always hope that what you've been waiting for is so much better than you thought. That risk is what makes the anticipation so exciting. I'd rather take the risk and see what happens." I smile at him, refusing to be disappointed about meeting cool people. That's my favorite part of moving around.

My anxiety makes me go over every hitch of my words as he stares at me, aggressively searching for something in my eyes. Should I step back? What the hell…

"Sorry to take my dear wife back." As Cain slides around Declan, I clear my throat and step back, feeling caught in Declan's stare. "But we better get back to work." Cain places his hand on the small of my back, helping me disengage from whatever the hell Declan did to me. My skin won't cool down and my heart slams against my chest, but I give them another tight smile before heading towards the door. As we leave, the three of them all share this nod that makes me feel like I missed an inside joke.

"See you soon, B…" Micah calls after us but gets cut off when Cain and I walk back into the loading center.

"Thanks for coming to get me. Those two wouldn't shut up." Cain guides me through the piles of stock while keeping his hand on my back, bringing my attention to the fact that I'm still wearing his jacket. This definitely seems intimate, but if we're all going to be friends, I'm not going to make him uncomfortable with my assumptions.

"They don't come off as chatty. But I like them." *I bet watching you guys demolish houses would be hot as fuck.* I save that bit for myself.

After sliding off his jacket, I give it to him, but he puts his hand right back onto me, making me walk a bit straighter. Maybe I just live in my head too much and the risk still needs to be gambled!

My shoulders come down in relief when we get to the shed. Walking through the mall with him touching my back didn't seem like a lot, but it felt heavy. I'm probably reading too much into it again. When we get inside, I go right to his present, knowing if I hesitate for a second, I'll talk myself out of it.

"The guys have plenty to say. But only with people they trust. That just happens to be few and far between." He leans on the table again with his knees spread like he always does.

"I prefer it that way too." I clear my throat to rid the apprehension choking me as I turn around with his gift in my hands. "I got you something. I know we didn't talk about it, and it's completely fine if you didn't get me something. I just thought of this and…had some free time. I thought you'd like it, I guess. I don't know if that's weird, but…" I push it towards him as I bite the inside of my cheek to shut myself up. Be cool for once.

He stands abruptly, forcing me to take a step back as my eyes widen. Not saying a word, his smile drops from his face as he snatches the gift from my hands. As he carefully unwraps the paper, I cringe in the silence he's cornering me in.

When he pulls out the small picture frame, his playful attitude vanishes from his face as he stares at the drawing I made him. My flat mate back in Chicago was going to art school, so I got to learn a bit from her, but every second he stays quiet, I fight not to speak or take it back from him, knowing it looks horrific. This is torture.

"It's the first ink the three of us got." He places a hand on his collar bone, the place where the tattoo of the three headed snake is. All his tattoos seem to tell a story, but that one is my favorite.

I go to speak, but only a shriek escapes me when he roughly grabs my face and slams his lips to mine. *Finally.* I swing my arms around his neck as he encircles my middle. Why haven't we been talking like this the entire time?

He spins me around to press me against the table as he slides his knee between my legs, his tongue surging with mine as we both groan into each other, gripping and pulling anything we can. *Holy shit.* He slides his hand over my hip, slipping into the bottom of my sweater to feel my skin, pulsing flames through me. My leg lifts against him as he pushes into me, my body aching to have him.

"Wait…" I press my palm against his chest to break the kiss, letting us both catch our breath. He doesn't let go of me, instead only pushing his thigh against mine. It goes against every instinct I have, but I go up on my toes to lean away. "We have to work." I struggle to get the words out because all I want to do is beg him to take me. His eyes blaze into me as he slides his tongue across his teeth, looking violently conflicted as he backs away from me.

"I'm sorry…" He shakes his head like he's as surprised as me that we got here. "Thank you for this." He holds up the picture gripped tightly in his hand, his voice coming out ragged and strained.

"Quite a thank you," I say with no humor in my voice like I'd intended. After a second, I nod and motion for him to sit so I can rush through our makeup. He moves to where he usually sits, acting as he always does, but his face seems like a new man. His hardened eyes never leave mine as his lips stay parted, making him look *hungry.*

Keeping my tongue between my teeth, I robotically do his makeup and then my own, regulating each and every breath. Half of me wants to talk about the kiss while the other part just wants to play it cool like he is. I can't use my words!

When I'm done with my makeup, I start pinning my hair up and wrangling in my curls. This is usually the time he leaves to let me get changed before coming back in, but he's not leaving this time. Instead, he stays leaning on the table with his hands clasped on his lap.

Glancing over at him, I pinch my brows in confusion, but his stare has turned...ravenous. Without a word, he darts his eyes to my bag beside me. As I try to decipher if he really means for me to get undressed in front of him, I just start doing it. He can leave if he wants.

I repeat that a few times in my head to gather my nerves as I start taking off my layers, feeling like this is overwhelmingly intimate. His eyes drag over my thighs as I strip down to my bra and underwear. This lighting is harsh for so much exposed skin, but the powerfully heated glint in his eyes is making me want to take off everything and bare myself for him to devour. Before I can do it, he grabs my bag and takes out my dress.

"I have a gift for you as well." He stands a foot away from me as he scrunches up my dress to put it over my head. "I want you to meet me here at nine tonight."

"But the mall closes early. It'll be empty for...three hours by that time." The strained, fumbling words escape my suddenly dry mouth as I shrug on the dress and focus on straightening the bottom, needing to break our crushing eye contact.

"For weeks, I've been trying to see where you belong on my list..." Without hesitation, he slides his hand up to frame my jaw and tilt me up to him, his hand feeling cool against my blazing skin. "And I think you belong on the bad side with me. So, at nine, when the only people here will be us, come and get your gift, Aria." His soft request doesn't seem to leave any space for reasoning as he brushes his thumb across my lips, forcing my eyes to close. I'll leave work right now if he'd like.

After I nod, he grips me tightly for a second before letting go and starting to undress. Knowing I'm going to ruin my cool if I stay here another second, and the fact that we're already five minutes late, I rush outside to calm down the families waiting.

One of the elves is already here, giving me a dirty look for being late, probably assuming correctly what Cain and I were just doing. We're usually late because one of us can't stop talking but today, the elf is right in her suspicion.

As I speak with the first family, the kids all light up and scream, 'Santa' when Cain comes out and waves. How can he still be hot like this? Tonight cannot come fast enough. Neither of us know much about each other's past, but he's right…I belong on the bad side with him. I'm probably much worse for what I've done.

Chapter Six

Aria

After hightailing it to the bus to get home after work, not even waiting for Cain to walk me to the stop like he usually does, my muscles surge with energy and nerves. The whole ride home and every minute of getting ready, it never stops.

He might be intense, but I can't get enough of it. Everyone puts layers of lies between the real them and what they choose to show society. I get why a lot of people do it, and I'm not innocent of it either. I fake smiles and conversations every day. It's hard to put into words, but Cain feels real.

I haven't put down any roots since I ran away from home, so I don't feel that raw energy with anyone, the type of stability people only get when someone truly knows them. Cain doesn't know the real me, and he won't ever, but around him, I still feel that natural air.

After a long shower, I make sure to put in my best effort when it comes to my hair and makeup. I give myself the 'no makeup' look to support the illusion that I'm not obsessing over meeting him. How do I even get in? I guess I can use one of the side doors near the loading bay. It's going to be cold as hell though.

I just now realized he's asking me to spend Christmas Eve with him. Maybe he didn't realize that and he's going to bail. Should I text him? Damnit!

Pushing away my anxiety, I focus on just having this experience. If I wasn't excited and dressing up for this, I'd just be alone with my tv and books. I *should* get a cat.

Shaking my head to refocus, I tame my curls a bit so they fall down my back and don't look too frizzy. I make a mental note to wrap my hair so the weather doesn't destroy my work. I pick out this forest green, knitted sweater dress and thick, black tights to keep me warm. It also shows off my ass pretty nicely. This is my usual go-to outfit for dates in winter because it's comfy, and with a pair of brown boots, I look damn cute.

After I wrap my hair in a scarf and sling it around my neck, I pull on my coat and rush to leave, knowing I'll be catching the last bus of the night. I'll have to wait at the mall for a bit, but it'll give me some time to calm my racing heart. As my nerves creep up again, I make sure Jenna at least knows I'm doing something stupid. She texts back a picture of her and Eric relaxing on the couch with the caption 'Doing Christmas right. Get some girl,' which motivates me. I do need some.

My brain runs on over drive as I go through the vacant, snowy city. I've had some soul crushingly lonely Christmases, but this one has the chance of being kind of fun. Even if he doesn't show up and texts that he has a family thing or something, at least I took a risk.

After I get off the bus at the mall, the wind swirls the snow across the empty parking lot, sending a shiver up my spine. The harsh wind blows me towards the building, oddly seeming far too eager to get me inside. I shove away the random urge to defy the wind as I bolt across the parking lot, wanting to give into my wild side for a night. I scurry to get inside, away from the cold and the alarm bells in my head.

As I dash to the side door near the loading dock, I curl my coat around myself and tuck my head down. When I get inside, I shake the snow off me and dramatically shiver, but nerves prick my skin as soon as I realize how eerily silent this place is.

How much trouble am I really going to get in for doing this? Security is here, but I'm sure Cain could talk them out of reporting us. He charms everyone.

44

Taking my coat off, I drape it over my arm with my scarf before checking myself out in the camera of my phone. Thankfully, my hair and makeup held up alright.

Seeing the mall completely empty and dark, only lit up by a few red emergency lights on the ceiling, rises goosebumps over my arms. My boots echo off the floors as I stride down the shadowy halls, fighting to keep my cool.

When I round the first-floor balcony, an odd glow catches my eye. I glance over the railing to the bottom floor up to the long hallway where the enormous tree is, lighting up the vacant space around it, glowing even brighter with the lit candles surrounding it. My breath gets lodged in my throat when I see him sitting in the middle of the wide, burgundy chair, still wearing his red overalls with a black t-shirt underneath. When his eyes lock on mine, I can't hold down my beaming smile as I wave to him.

He's here!

"Now this, is quite a gift!" My shout echoes off the vast, empty hallways as I stifle my excited laughter and head over to the stairs. Even from this distance, I can see his smirk pull to the side.

"We actually had something a bit different in mind." As his deep, booming voice reaches me, my brows pinch in confusion.

"We?" The word is barely out of my mouth before two people emerge from behind the tree, rounding it to stand beside Cain. I can tell it's Micah and Declan dressed in their black security gear, their intimidating frames unmistakable. My feet stop when red flags and sirens go off in my mind. This isn't good.

"We're going to show you that what you've been waiting for was far better than what you thought." Declan's raspy tenor slithers across the distance, resonating around me. As my breath starts freezing in my throat, I have to grip the railing to steady myself.

"What do you think I've been waiting for?" I snap back when my irritation builds. This is some sketchy trap. Slipping my hand into my bag, I wrap my fingers around my phone, ready to call the cops if this is as bad as my nerves are telling me.

"You need to be set free, Baby!" Micah shouts as he throws his hands up in the air. "And we finally don't have to fucking wait anymore!" He lets out a terrifying laugh as he starts to pace back and forth in front of the other two, glaring at me the entire time, looking ready to attack.

"What are you talking about?" My voice cracks as fear grips my throat.

When Cain slowly stands from the chair, the three of them take a step closer to me, causing me to take one back, my nerves screaming at me to flee.

"It's time for us to truly introduce ourselves." Cain gestures wide in front of him as he grins again, only building the icy fear within me. "It's not going to be easy, but I think you should listen to yourself during this, Aria." He taps the side of his temple.

"So…if my brain is telling me to run…what should I do?" I force an awkward laugh to try and make light about how fucking creepy this is.

"Please run," Micah's murmur slinks towards me like a growl as he rolls his shoulders back and stops pacing, his sinister glare chilling me even from this far away.

They don't have to tell me twice. I don't waste another second before running away, pounding my boots on the floor to make it outside. When provoking laughter echoes off the walls, a whimper blasts out of my burning throat as fear wraps its glacial hands around me.

What the hell did I get myself into? The one time I do something crazy on Christmas, and I get presented with a nightmare. Just my luck.

When hard footsteps bang off the hallway behind me, I drop my coat so I can call the cops and keep running away. Turning down the hall towards the closest exit, I desperately pant for air and try to open my phone, but my hands are shaking too hard.

I drag in air when I finally make it to the doors and shove my body against it as I try to dial. At the same moment, I come to two dreadful realizations. There's no service on my phone, and the doors are chained from the outside. They've locked me in. I can already hear that one of them is too close for me to turn back around.

As I shove my phone into my bra in case I find a signal somewhere else, I glance behind me up the wide, darkened hallways as forceful steps reverberate towards me. Breathing through my adrenaline, I try to think of anything I can do to escape.

When I recognize Micah's frightening laughter, I dash into the huge bookstore to my right, one of the few stores I know that don't lock their gate to the hallway because it's also an emergency exit. Maybe the guys forgot to chain this door!

I don't know what's happening, but I need to get out. This will not be my last Christmas.

Chapter Seven
Aria

Trying to be quiet is damned near impossible when my breathing is so loud, but I can't stop the gasping cry that blasts off the tall ceilings as Micah lets out a roaring howl when he gets into the bookstore.

A loud crash rattles through the air when he knocks something over, getting closer every second. When I get to the doors, the moonlight glints off the chain on this one as well. Instead of wasting time to panic, I decide to hide.

Dashing up the few stairs to the next section, I dare a glance behind me and instantly regret it. Micah launches himself over a table, scattering books to the ground before eating up the distance between us with his long strides.

"Leave me alone!" I scream as I turn back around to keep running, knowing that the dark intentions behind his menacing glare aren't a joke. As I frantically look for something to fight him off with, my foot catches on the last step, sending me stumbling forward.

I know I'm too late before he even grabs me. I spin around, ready to slam my fist into him, but he's on me! He groans out a chuckle as he shoves me, slamming my back against a stack of books and sending some of them to the ground.

"What the hell do you think you're doing?" I put my hands up to claw his eyes, but he grabs them and pins both of my wrists above me, surging his body closer to trap me. I bring my knee up to crush his balls, but he quickly puts his feet between mine before pushing my legs apart to stop me. I squirm as much as I can, but it's like fighting against a steel

49

cage! "Please, Micah…" Before I can continue, he puts my wrists in one of his unyielding hands so he can slap his other one over my mouth.

As his wide manic eyes drill into mine, a blast of heated pressure pushes into my stomach, twisting with fear and confusion.

"I've listened to you for months. Every fucking word, Baby," he groans harshly as he dives his face to my neck before taking a long, slow inhale. "But you've never said my name before. I knew it would sound so *fucking* good."

I curse at him from behind his hand as I try to twist out of his grasp, but I'm starting to realize fighting is useless. It's easy to tell that the three of them work out a lot, but the strength he has is far more than I expected. As if he's used to chasing and catching people like this.

My brain refuses to work properly to give me another plan when he drags his hand from my mouth down to my neck. His lips brush against my skin with the softness of a lover, but his bruising grip on my wrists only tightens as his firm chest presses into me.

"Please tell me what's going on," I whimper out as he presses his thumb into my chin to turn my face away before sliding his tongue along the burning skin on my neck. The growling moan that rises from his throat spikes my panic even higher, slamming my heart against my ribs.

"Cain and Declan make the plans. I was just happy to be along for the ride when we got hired here," he murmurs his low reasoning against me. "But then we saw you…and I could tell right away that you were made for us." His hips press into me, trembling my knees, but I'm still trapped against the bookshelf with his solid frame. "But the guys weren't ready to admit it. I had to wait even longer for you." The frustrated grunt that vibrates through him tightens his muscles along his steely limbs.

I try to make sense of his words, but when he opens his mouth on the side of my throat, sending a pulse of pressure into me, I slam my eyes shut as my mind starts to boil along with my skin. Still holding my hands above me with one hand, he trails his other down my side to bunch up my dress. I try so hard not to fight back just yet, hoping my tactic of keeping him talking will work until I figure out how to get away.

Since his neck is right next to my mouth, I could maybe take a chunk out of him, but he might hit me or worse if I don't take a good enough bite. I need to be smart about this one.

"What did I do?" I tighten my lips to hold down my cry as he pulls my dress up over my ass and grips me tight, his hips pushing me against the bookshelf until more of them crash to the ground beside us.

"You were just *you*. When we got hired to take out that scumbag, Kurt, you were there…waiting for us."

"What did you do with Kurt?" I gasp as I squirm again, but I regret it in seconds when he slaps his hand back over my mouth and leans his head away. I would be relieved that he's not touching me or dragging his tongue over me anymore, but the suddenly furious glint in his eyes offers no relief.

"Don't you dare say another man's name when my hands are on you unless you want them shredded!" he roars right into my face as he digs his fingers into my jaw. When I rapidly nod, terrified of what he might do, his demeanor immediately switches back to ravenous desire as his brows pull in and his grip lessens. "Let's not fight anymore. I have too many things to show you."

He holds my jaw as he crashes his demanding mouth back onto my neck, sending a rolling beat straight to my center, but I try to force that away. My traitorous body has always pushed me towards danger, but this is too much. Before I can tell him to fuck off, his hand snaps down between my legs to rip a huge hole in my tights. I take in a crying shriek when his hand slams back on top of my underwear.

"Kurt was nothing. He hurt people, innocent people. Then I gutted him and buried him in a landfill. Don't give him a second thought."

"You killed him?" I re-up my struggles as much as I can, twisting and wriggling to get away, but he spins me around to shove my front into the shelf, pressing my cheek against the wood as he grips my hair.

"I know! Don't be mad…" The remorseful glint that sneaks into his vicious tone doesn't fool me for a second. "Cain refused to tell you about our business until you were ready. But I told them you'd understand. You think the evil ones should die screaming. Don't you? My bad girl." He rips my dress up over my ass again before delivering a stinging slap. As he groans out a rough curse and digs his fingers into my hip, I stifle my shriek as fire slices through me from his frantic manipulations of my body.

"You don't know me." I thrust my elbow into him, but he molds his chest to my back, shoving the air out of my lungs. I gasp again when his hard shaft presses right against my stinging ass.

"Oh, I know you. I was the first to see you. Our *Queen*." He pulls my dress down over my shoulder before pressing his mouth back against my blazing skin. "I tried to show the guys what you were, how you were perfect for us," he mutters coarsely against my skin. "It took them some time, but now we all see the truth. You're next." When I try to shove him back, he grabs my wrist and stretches my arm up before grinding against me, as if he's well prepared for me to keep fighting. *Holy shit.*

"I'm your nothing," I stifle my cry, refusing to let these maniacs see me break!

"Don't fucking lie to me!" His hand whips around me to encircle my throat, trapping my breath inside me. "You know you don't belong with these exhausting *people*." He releases my throat, letting me take in another breath, but it freezes in my lungs again when he drags his hand down my chest and spreads his fingers out over my abdomen. "You were meant to live in the underbelly of this society. The rules are harsher, the judgement is fierce, and you'll fucking thrive there, Aria. You feel that. You can fight, but don't lie to yourself. We both know you haven't found where you belong yet." His hand trails lower as his voice softens to a caress.

Squeezing my eyes shut, I realize trying to reason with him is as useless as fighting is. They're all insane. As every crime show I've ever watched runs through my head, a few ideas pop up.

"Okay, Micah," I whisper, trying to calm him down. "Let's talk about this. I'm afraid. Please..." I try to keep my voice level to make him see me as more than this fantasy he's created.

"You had to be scared to see the truth," he whispers against my ear as he trails his hand down my body to cup my pussy over my underwear again. I go up on my toes to get away from him, but all that does is drag my ass against his terrifyingly hard shaft. "Tell me the truth...no one's ever made you feel in more control over your fear, have they? And this is the first time you've liked running away and hiding...haven't you?" His words hit me like a punch, but his heated hand over my pussy keeps enough of my focus to be able to ignore him. "And I'm willing to bet that no one's been able to make you this wet...have they?" Before I can truly register what he said, he quickly twists his fingers, pushing my underwear aside and gliding through my lips, letting me know instantly that I'm wet. Damnit.

Shaking my head, I try to think of anything else to say to make him release me, but as his harsh groan rattles his chest against me, my thoughts have a harder time keeping up with my fear and utterly inappropriate arousal.

"I've never experienced torture like the agony I felt waiting to find out what you taste like." Still holding my arms above me, he presses his face beside mine and brings his wet fingers up to his mouth. My eyes widen as his flutter close when he slides his fingers past his lips. The needy moan that erupts from his throat has me squeezing my thighs together as another wave of heat hits me. This is nuts.

Suddenly, he grabs me and spins me again. I don't even have time to correct my feet before he crushes his lips against mine, rolling his tongue into my mouth to twirl with my own, mixing our tastes. My idiot brain stays shut off for just a second as heat swells from low in my stomach, pulling my muscles across my bones.

When he presses his forehead to mine, his blue eyes keep me hypnotized as we breathe in each other's air.

"I know your fear because it's my own. We're one, Baby." His strong hands grip my sweater as he pushes us together like he's trying to absorb me, his firm demands continuing to keep me useless. But my mind catches up when I realize he didn't step in between my feet again.

As hard as I can, my knee launches up, hitting him right in the groin. He barks out a pained groan as he staggers back and drops one knee to catch his breath. I'm stunned for only a second, but when he coughs out a taunting chuckle, I snap back to the moment. Knowing I only have another second, I sprint away, not slowing down for anything.

"I told you! My bad girl likes to fight!" His booming voice follows me as I dash out of the store, reminding me of my dire situation…there are two other lunatics here.

Micah is out of his fucking mind, but he's right about one thing. If they're going to assault or kill me like they seemingly did to Kurt, I'm going down with a fight. They're not the only killers in this mall.

Chapter Eight
Aria

I don't know if I can hear anything over the blood rushing through my ears, but I'm pretty sure the other two are downstairs still. Hoping that's true, I take the side stairs up to the third level.

As soon as I get to the top, I take off my boots and run in my ripped tights instead so I don't make any noise. I try to slip into a sunglasses store that I know has a small office in the back where I could hide, but the metal gate into the hallway is locked. When I hear a door slam from behind me, I stifle my shriek as I side-step further down the hall towards the furniture department store.

Once I get inside, every sound reverberates louder with the tall ceilings, so I slow my pace and quiet my breathing even more. I can barely see anything in here, the red emergency lights being the only illumination around, but I think it's the perfect place to hide. Rushing past the kitchen section, I take a quick detour to find a display knife block. I rip one out and hold it close to me as I run deeper into the store.

When I get to the bedroom section, I find a huge wardrobe and rush inside before closing myself in. Holding the knife in both hands, I try desperately to calm my heartbeat, taking in long inhales through my nose that burn my throat and quickly breathing them out through my mouth.

My hands shake as I press one of them against my mouth when I hear pounding footsteps rushing past me. It's more than one of them. Shit! I only risk leaning my head a bit to the left so I can see a sliver of what's happening through the crack in the door.

"Damn. I thought she came in here. She's quick." Cain's smoky voice makes me squeeze my eyes shut as fury blasts into me. How could I have been so wrong about him?

"I'll sweep the rest of the area up here. You check downstairs. Micah's on the main floor. He thinks she's going back to the loading dock." Declan's deep baritone creeps through the air towards me, forcing my eyes to open again. Maybe I can take him out first if he's choosing to stay alone up here. But I won't lose my location just yet.

I can see the edge of Declan's tall frame as he shoves Cain's shoulder. As he jogs away, he leaves a lasting, horrifying impression of his echoing suggestive laugh. I expect Declan to start aggressively searching for me, but he doesn't move yet.

Slowly, he takes off his jacket with all the pockets and straps, leaving him in only a black shirt pulled tight across his chest, revealing his darkly inked arms.

"I know you're here, Butterfly." His eerie tone makes me dig my teeth into my tongue to stop from whimpering in fear. He carefully removes his gloves and tosses them onto the bed beside him where he put his jacket. "I know you must be confused. But this is necessary. You're in too much denial about who you really are." He shakes his head as he slides his hands into the pockets of his black cargo pants before strolling out of sight.

The need to scream back at him and remind them all that they don't know shit about me arises, but I push it down, knowing I have to continue being smart about this.

"We were just here to eliminate some filth, but when Micah almost lost his mind over you, I figured Cain and I would have to drag him out of this awful city." His voice trails away from me, letting me take another filling breath, but his steps slowly return on the other side of the wardrobe I'm around…like he's circling me. "For him, waiting is akin to death, so when he agreed to wait for us to *see* you, we knew he was serious." The low, throaty chuckle seems to seep through the thin wood around me, as if he can see right through. "You were…alluring, so I was tempted to learn more," he murmurs a few feet from me, tightening every muscle across my chest as I try desperately not to make a sound. "It turns out…he was right. It's not the mystical bullshit he spews, but even though you've suppressed parts of your personality to be able to blend, you truly are perfect, for each of us." He lets out a long sigh before finally stepping away, letting me fill my lungs. "You're wild and sadistic enough to keep Micah on your tail, giving you the power needed to steady him. You crave to be worshipped, which provides Cain with a purpose," he states definitely as if reading off a resume. "And you long for stability and strength to exist among the chaos and violence of this life…which is all I've ever wanted as well." When he saunters in front of the wardrobe, I grip my knife tightly in both hands, ready to do some damage if he realizes where I am.

Squeezing my eyes shut for a moment, I attempt to shove away his words and chalk them up to being the ramblings of a psychopath, just like I did with Micah. It's like trying to shove a feral cat into a carrier though.

"But even though I realized what the guys were telling me, you were still my butterfly who thought she was a little bug." He lets out a heavy breath with a hint of frustration, but I have to ignore the ache in his tone along with his words. They don't know me. "If this was going to work, we need to rip that cocoon off you, make you realize that you're the one holding yourself back. I should have found you sooner, but it's time to stop running."

"Enough with this bullshit! Save your stupid metaphors for each other! You're just going to hurt me, and you're trying to make it poetic. Fuck all of you!" The words explode out of me as I slam my hand against the back of the wardrobe, but I flinch away with a gasping shriek when I realize what I did. My eyes close as I shove my fists into them in shame for not being able to control myself.

"You're right. We will hurt you," the smoky, amused chuckle that trickles out of him raises the icy fear in my body to new, staggering levels. "Changing your life is painful, but you don't trust anyone enough to hurt for them yet. You're going to trust me though, quicker than you're prepared for..." The silence after his words sits so heavy on me that it's harder to breathe every second. I know he's just beyond the flimsy doors beside me, but he's still far enough away that I'll be able to fight. "Before you do what you're thinking, why don't you come out so I can show you what I mean. Or you can fight and scream, and I'm sure Micah will come running, ready to rip you apart too soon. Would you rather that?"

My fists shake around the knife as I silently scream my fury at him. I don't really have an option here, but I won't be manipulated into trusting him with the threat of his attack dog!

Tightening my features, I open the door and crawl out. Keeping the knife in my hand, I stand, ready to face him, but he's gone. My confidence drowns in terror as I'm presented with nothing but darkness around me, only slightly lit up by the red lights on the ceiling.

I'm barely able to hold down my scream when he appears beside me and grabs my wrist at the knife. I go to claw his eyes with my other hand, but he spins me around and forces me to walk forward with both hands behind my back.

I squirm in frustration, but I stay quiet, knowing two of them will truly render me useless. When he shifts me to the next section where a dining room display is set up, he presses me down on a long, wooden table, softly placing my chest to the cool wood. I jolt back with a gasp, but I still lean down on it, glad for the relief on my singeing skin.

"What do you think you were going to do with this?" He yanks the knife out of my hand and stabs it into the wood next to my face, ripping every one of my nerves to attention as a harsh shriek rushes into me, unfortunately stilling my trembling muscles. "Oh, no. I'd be quieter than that. You and I need some time alone." He drags a chair in behind me before forcing me to sit, keeping a firm grasp on my shoulder.

I want to stay discreet, but I'm not willing to miss a chance, so I reach forward to grab the knife, but he holds me back. Not eager to deal with more than one of them at a time, I snap my furious glare up to him to whisper yell, "What was I going to do with the knife? Fucking kill all three of you assholes. I don't know what you *think* you're doing with me, but I'm done playing this little game. Let me go." I cross my arms over my chest, trying to hide how truly terrified I am of his shadowy, looming frame above me.

Letting go of my shoulder, lean his hip on the table beside me, casually gliding around me without fear of what I might do. The low, red light glinting off his amused smirk makes it easier to hide my fear as rage overtakes it. They're just playing with me.

When he starts sliding his hand up his thigh, I try to hold his glare but fail when I realize he's pulling a long switchblade out of his pocket. Hiding my fear becomes a bit harder as he expertly flips it open, shimmering the light off the sharp edge and locking every one of my nerves in place. The air in my lungs rushes out of me when he whips the tip of the blade right to my face.

Christmas' top story will be, '*Merry Christmas folks, the mall will be closed while we clean the remains of missing girl.*' My family will think this is justice.

"You really want me to let you go?" He twists the knife slowly, almost dragging the edge over my jawline. Fighting the urge to try ripping his hand away in fear I might die, I tighten my lips and nod. "Then I'll make you a deal. You listen to me like the good girl I know you can be, and I'll let you run again." He taps the tip of the blade against my chin, and I nod again without thinking about it for too long and losing my nerve, not having another clue what to do in this situation. Using his knife, he tilts me up to him as he leans down, bringing his stern face inches away from mine and spreading warmth over my skin with his heated breath. "Grip the arms of the chair and spread your knees. Do, not, move. Understood?" Averting my gaze as my muscles start quivering in waves, I nod once again, but he pushes the tip harder against me, forcing my attention back to him. "Oh no, Butterfly. I'll need your words."

Even though they grate against my burning throat, I force words out as I grip the arms of the chair, my thighs quivering as I try to spread them. "I understand, Declan." His lips twitch, his features roughening into anger as he presses the blade into my skin, sending a sharp ache through me.

"You're too good to use that name I was given. When I've earned it…you will only call me, Sir." He stares unblinking at me, the tip of his blade piercing into me, waiting for my response. "Are you ready?" he asks tenderly as he drags the blade down my neck, leaving a trail of sharp fire.

Intense had nothing on these men. I'm pretty sure some more horrific shit is about to happen, but if I don't end up in the news, this Christmas will still be…memorable.

Closing my eyes, I nod again to answer him, ready to face the repercussions of the situation I've gotten myself into.

"What did I say?" He grabs my hair with his free hand before yanking my head back, the sting of pain making me slam my eyes closed as heat pulses through me again. Damnit. "Use your words, Butterfly." His raspy tone does nothing to quell the traitorous fire inside my body.

"I'm ready. I'll…be good," I whisper, forcing myself not to curse at him as I lean back and spread my knees to the side, rising the bottom of my dress. Leisurely, he shakes his head as he releases me and draws the knife back, his cold grin pulling to the side as he flicks his belt buckle open.

He rips his belt through the holes, sending an ominous crack through the silence. After placing his knife between his teeth, he loops the belt through the lock, his precise, stern movements pulling every ounce of my attention.

The survivalist inside me yells at me to grab the knife that's still lodged in the table in front of me, but I don't think antagonizing him is the right move here. I don't have much time to even think of that before he flips the belt in front of my face, pressing it against my lips and prompting me to open my mouth.

It goes against everything inside me, but I eventually part my lips, and he tightens the belt around my face, forcing me to spread my teeth around the leather. I clutch the arms of the chair as fear, rage, and an exhilarating fire twist up my muscles. They haven't rambled about killing me yet, so…maybe I still have time.

"I don't want to hear a single fucking thing after that," he whispers against my ear as he leans behind me, putting his face next to mine. I hurriedly nod, having no clue what the next minute holds, but shamefully, I want to know.

I can't wrap my head around them killing Kurt, which I don't even feel the need to call the cops about. I just *feel* like he deserved it. Everyone thought he was sweet. If they came to me yesterday and admitted it, I'd be having a much different reaction.

Have I truly just met three guys I would have wanted to buy a drink for prior to them being psychotic stalkers? Why didn't they just ask me out for dinner? I told myself before I left my apartment that I didn't care how this night turned out, and even though this outcome wasn't on my radar, I think I'm making the smartest moves I can. I can handle one of them, and I think Declan is the one that can restrain the rabid hound sniffing below us.

He whips his arms around me before roughly grabbing the front of my dress at my chest and slicing the knife through it, splitting the fabric to either side and letting my phone fall out of my bra onto the floor. I curse at him from behind the belt, but I don't move.

"Your body has been begging for our eyes. Our touch…" He flips the knife over to tap the tip of it against my lips, pushing me into his shoulder as I tremble between him and the blade.

As he looms behind me and rests his arms around my shoulders over the chair, he softly glides his knuckle across my collar bone and trails the flat of the blade over my front. When he curls the sharp tip around one of my breasts over my bra and down my quivering stomach, he slides his hand over the side of my throat to tilt me back.

"I want you to show me how strong you are." He glides the blade over my thighs, quickening my breathing as my jaw flexes on the belt. What the hell am I doing?

Suddenly, he winds back and stabs the knife down sideways into the wood between my thighs. My body instinctively jerks away, but he doesn't let me move. Still keeping his grip on the knife, he slips behind me and slides his other hand down my chest, trapping me between his arms. When he slips into my underwear through my wet lips without warning, I go to grab his hand with a gasp, but I manage to stay somewhat still by clasping the arms of the chair.

"You're going to keep those legs spread for me. You break my rules, you get cut." He slides his fingers along my clit, pinching it lightly. Even that small touch has my body arching and rolling under his arms. *Traitor!*

I wrap my foot around the leg of the chair when my thighs start trembling, but it only gets worse when he slides two fingers around my clit through my lips, forcing my attention to his powerful hands working me over. As my legs jerk in response, my thigh presses against the side of the knife as the other one quivers faster. He teases my clit before sliding down to my entrance and spreading my arousal over me, his firm arms constricting my chest against the chair.

I feel like I'm starting to ignite as I feast on his skillful control over my body, but I try to tell myself that it's just my own terror raising my adrenaline and clouding my judgment. I just have…no choice. At that thought, I moan out against the belt as my eyes roll, taking my head back with it.

"God, you're so fucking perfect." He lifts his hand before slapping it down on my clit, tugging each of my muscles tight. I yelp against the belt between my teeth as he slides his lips towards my ear and circles his fingers over my clit, every touch he's giving me only raising my temperature. *Fuck.*

Both my thighs quiver against the blade between them before I force them back to the side. I have to dig my hands fingers into the wooden arms as my impulses try reaching out to grab my legs.

When he slides two fingers inside me, he gently strokes my walls as I whine for more. A reasonable part of my brain tries to yell at my logic, knowing this is too messed up, even for me. I've never experienced this. Usually, the guys I've been with are too afraid to try anything rough with me, but I didn't even know most of them that well.

This is an entirely new level of fucked up for me though. I try to comfort myself, telling my logic that he won't actually let me get cut, but that gets washed away when he lets the knife go, shaking it against me a bit and scraping my skin.

"You've been waiting so long for someone to end your charade. Begging for me to find you and make you my little whore." He pushes my underwear down and uses the knife to slide through them before tossing them away.

Before I can take a breath, both his hands are on my pussy, one sliding his fingers inside me while the other rhythmically circles my clit. I try to stifle my moan, but it's drowned out by his raspy growl against my neck. My eyes widen at the knife between my legs as every ounce of crippling worry outside of this moment vanishes.

As a blast of pressure hits my core, building quicker than I can catch up, I lean into his arms around me for some kind of anchor to reality as he drags his teeth along my throat, leading to where my neck meets my shoulder. Somehow knowing he's about to bite me, my muscles coil up in preparation, pressing both my thighs against the blade. My skin bends around the sharp edges, but it doesn't cut in.

"Do you see how good you can feel when you stop hiding who you are? We want every fucking part of you." He widens his mouth with a hungry groan before digging his teeth into me, searing a shot of harsh fire through me.

As he furiously rubs my clit and curls his fingers inside me, the pain viciously mixes with pleasure, slamming my orgasm into me. It rolls up my body and quakes my legs, slicing the blade against my upper thigh. The sharp flames wick at my skin from the cut, but my chest arches against his biceps as I ground out a rumbling hum when another fiery pulse throbs through me.

He never stops his movements as my walls clench down on his fingers and my legs shudder together again, giving me another cut. The pain aggressively builds every other sensation within me as my teeth dig into the leather, a muffled cry scorching my throat.

As he slows, I'm finally able to take in a few panting breaths as my muscles go slack. I gradually unclench my fists from jabbing into the wood so hard. He unhooks the belt so he can drop it around my neck as I take in a huge, ragged inhale. After he tightens the belt, pressing the cool leather against the boiling skin on my throat, he holds the long end in his hand while stepping around me.

"What the hell was that?" I track him with my gaze while my brain reboots, refusing to accept that was a simple orgasm.

"That…is what good girls deserve." He settles his grip on the belt that's basically a leash now before tugging it towards him, forcing me to lean forward as he lifts his fingers to wrap his lips around them, tasting me. An entirely new ache inside me pulses; a ravenous, violent ache.

When he rips the knife out of the chair, I cringe back, pulling against the belt and tightening it even more around my throat, constricting my airflow. After he presses the tip of the blade into the table, he retracts it and slips it back into his pocket, never taking his eyes off me. As he leans down to bring his face to mine, he brushes his knuckles over my knee, heading to the lines of blood trailing over my thigh.

I'm not sure I understand it yet, but it feels as if I can catch my breath and restore my nerves if I only focus on listening to him, not moving a single muscle unless told to. Nothing else matters for a second. I think my orgasm made me stupid. They're dangerous.

My eyes flutter closed as he drags his knuckles through my cuts, but I force myself to watch him slowly trail his tongue over his finger to taste more of me. His unwavering gaze flickers with starved aggression for just a moment as a harsh curse resounds through him.

"There's not a drop of you that doesn't taste like fucking paradise," he rumbles deep in his throat before snapping his hand to my jaw and yanking me up off the chair. When his lips crash against mine, he instantly wraps his tongue around me. *Where did these men come from?*

I can't stop my arms from coiling around his middle to grip his shirt, needing reassurance that he's real, and not some manifestation of all the dark desires I've ever had. When my logic finally comes back, I shove off him, staggering away a few steps as I rip the belt off my neck. My eyes widen as I glare my accusations at him and catch my breath. They're here to hurt my body, but they won't damage my walls.

"Run fast, *Butterfly*. It'll make the catch that much sweeter." His threatening words stay with me as I rush away. My dress is in shreds around my body, my tights are ripped open, I don't have any underwear, and on top of all of that, I truly think I'm losing my mind.

Chapter Nine
Aria

My muscles are starting to turn to jelly. Between the running, the adrenaline, and the mystifying sensations they're imposing on me, I don't know how much longer I can keep going.

Once I get to the main floor, instead of running, I sneak along the shadows, focusing my hearing and trying to keep my head level. My phone is gone, my clothes are torn, and I don't even have shoes, but I still need to get out.

I feel like I'm not only fighting all three of them, but also my own body now, that bitch. When I hear a loud bang behind me, I freeze in a darkened alcove between two stores.

"Baby! Let me make it up to you!" Micah's foreboding tone bounces off the walls in every direction. Knowing I'm not in a good vantage point right now, I keep edging along the walls and metal gates, waiting for the moment I'm going to have to run again. *"I hear your bleeding...did you like it?"* His pitch lowers as he closes in on me, but I still don't think he knows where I am. I'm not sure where he is either. He could be above me for all I know. Every shadow, every gleam of light...everything is a threat.

When his words register, I glance down at the cuts along my thighs, but they're not bleeding any more. Crimson is smeared over my skin though, reminding me of everything Declan did to me. Shaking my head, I try ridding the ache that memory brings.

A snarling breath makes me snap my head to the left again. Next to one of the kiosks in the middle of the hallway is a new shadow, tall, lithe, and dangerous. *Micah.*

All of a sudden, every fact I know about this mall rushes through me. All the closest exits, the stairs, the main entrance, and which stores are closest.

Giving up on staying quiet, my feet rush along the floor to the shoe store about fifty feet in front of me where the closer always forgets to lock his gate. He's hung out with Jenna and me a few times, and his boss always gets him in trouble for forgetting the padlock.

Micah's taunting laugh rattles from behind me as his boots slam against the floor, spiking my heart rate once again, but I don't slow down. Praying that the shoe store guy forgot to lock the gate again, I launch myself at the entrance, sobbing out a sigh of relief when it opens for me.

I can't quiet the winded screech that rushes into me as I scramble to lock it behind me, my hands aggressively shaking as I hook the lock around the metal. As his crashing footsteps bang closer, my limbs quiver with fear in response.

As soon as I click the lock closed, Micah launches himself at the gate, throwing me backwards. I crash against the front table filled with shoes, but he can't get me now.

"*Fuck*, every second I think you can't possibly be sexier, you prove me wrong," he growls deep in his throat as his quaking fists grip the gate, his feral eyes devouring my exposed skin. Wrapping my shredded dress around myself, I glare at him and take a step forward, my confidence soaring now that there's a barrier between us.

"Leave me the fuck alone! You've played your little game. We're done now." Reaching behind me, I grab a high heel and hold it up to him, hoping I seem as threatening as I feel.

"We'll never be done, Baby." He shakes his head as his face screws up in confusion and pain. "I thought you realized that by now. You'll never get away from me!" He slams his hand to the gate, rattling the metal against the lock, his mood still switching each second.

"I told you we had to be patient with her, boys." Cain's smoky tenor slithers around Micah as he tilts into sight, leaning against the other side of the entrance of the store, just beyond the gate.

"You said it was time." Micah's tone turns into a sinister warning as he drags his fingers down the metal.

"She sees the truth. She's still lying to herself." Declan strolls in behind them and leans on the back of one of the benches in the middle of the hallway. The eerie silence of the empty mall fills with my panicked breathing now that I'm confronted with the three of them, the metal gate between us seeming pathetic.

"How dare you assume anything about me." I step forward again, pointing the high heel at them all as I narrow my eyes. "You three are killers, right? Fucking psychopaths! And now, you're just going to hurt me until I submit and become your plaything? I will stab, bite, and rip each of you apart before that ever happens!" I raise the heel in my hand, hoping my shaky voice still comes out like the promise it is.

"You're right. We *are* killers, Aria. And we started young." Cain's brows pull in as he slides his hands into his pockets. "That's why we saw who you really were. You're just like us." The side of his lips lift again like they have before, but his inviting charm only builds my fear instead of making me melt. They can't know the truth...can they?

"You took your first life the same age as I did," Micah groans deep in his throat as he tightens his grip on the metal. "Tell me everything. I've read every news article about your uncle's death...but I think you did something before you set the fire. Am I right? Tell me, Baby." He digs his teeth into his lip as he presses his forehead against the gate.

The high heel drops to the ground as I slap my hands over my mouth, the tears I've been holding back forcing themselves out. I shake my head, not having the words to deny the truth. No one knows what I did.

"Wait! Don't tell me yet!" Micah slams his hand against the metal again before taking a step away and rolling his shoulders back. "Tell me when my cock is buried deep inside you." His words force the air in my lungs to freeze as I back up another step. "You're ripping my heart out, Aria! Open the fucking gate!" He starts pacing as he loses his cool, his temper spiking and falling as he shakes the gate like the maniac he is.

"Take a walk," Declan demands, not removing his eyes from me.

"I'll be back. And I'll make it up to you," Micah coos as he brushes his knuckles against the metal. With a wink, he takes off, running into the shadows and laughing out in triumph. He yells something about the Queen, but his echo is too muffled to make out beyond his ominous tone.

"I may have killed him…" I swallow down the pain that those words bring, never having spoken them before. "But it's not like I made a job out of it. He was…a monster. He deserved it." I squeeze my eyes shut to rid myself of the memories of him. Horrible, vile, agonizing memories.

"I know, my love," Cain whispers as he curls his tatted fingers through the gate. When my eyes lock with him, I get a wave of energy like he really does know. Not just what I went through, but how it changes a person.

That same sensation…that real, raw energy starts pulling me towards him again. Shit. I really am going to break.

"We know better than anyone that it's easier to run and hide…" Declan gestures to my hideaway around us as he slowly strides towards me, his hand stained with my blood, his eyes slicing past more of my skin. "That's why, even though I believe you're our 'Queen,' perfectly made for us, I thought we would have to leave you. You'd already dealt with enough evil in this life."

I turn my back to them, feeling more vulnerable than I've ever experienced. Curling my arms around myself, I sniffle back tears, not willing to let them see my walls shatter.

"That's why we decided I would get close to you, push you a little." Cain picks up where Declan stopped, his smooth nature swirling around me like an embrace. "And every time I showed you a hint of who I was, of who we are, you only fought harder to be close to me. I understand it's scary, but you belong *with* us," he murmurs the truth of what I've been denying the past few weeks. "All of us snuff out the monsters of this world. The only difference between you and the three of us, is that we get paid to do it." His pitch takes on an amused glint, adding gasoline to the rage brewing inside me.

Rolling laughter erupts from my throat as my head falls back. I'm such an idiot. Why didn't I see the truth? They made it so damn obvious. I kept giving them the benefit of the doubt, defending them to everyone, saying they were just odd or intense, but they were shoving the facts right into my face. They joked about contracts they've taken for fuck's sake. *Freelancers.*

For the first time in years, my shoulders feel light as the pain in my back subsides. I've held the truth of what happened to my family for the past fourteen years. The authorities reported that I died in the fire I set, but I knew they were looking for me. My parents died when I was young, but my family, mainly my sadistic uncle, was extremely wealthy and influential in our city. No one dared defy him, until I took matters into my own hands.

And then I was just some twelve-year-old kid on the run, conning schools into believing I belonged there, moving to the next town before anyone got suspicious, and mostly living in malls where I could steal and sneak around all I wanted. I was always gone before someone could spot me.

It was exhausting, lonely, sometimes terrifying, but not the *hell* I was in before. I never stopped running. Changed my last name, never stayed anywhere too long…never belonged. And the first time I felt like someone knew me, someone was understanding me, it was three insane hitmen. Of course.

"Are you guys fucking serious? What were you thinking? Have you never met a woman before?! Why didn't you start it off with, '*Hey Aria, looks like we're all fucked up. Wanna go on a date?*'" Spinning around, I throw my arms out wide, letting my dress fall off me completely. If they really know who I am and what I did…then I'm done hiding. It's killing me.

My aggressive tone and the fact that I'm bared to them makes both of them stand up straight, their shoulders stiff as they glare at me. My fury and confidence booming, I take a step closer, narrowing my eyes at them.

"You're all so screwed in the heads that you thought stalking me, manipulating me, trapping me, and then assaulting me was how to go about getting my attention?" I shout my frustrations as I rip off the rest of my tights and throw it at them.

"You never told us to stop." Cain slams his hand against the gate, anger cracking through his usually relaxed façade.

"Don't pretend like that matters!" I thrust my accusing finger towards him. "My brain and my body can disagree. You lied to me for weeks! Made me think I was going nuts!" I slam my hand on the gate between us, but it only pulls him in closer. "And *you* touched what wasn't yours!" I stomp over to Declan as I raise my chin and harden my severe scowl. His shoulders expand as he narrows his eyes into slits, completing his transformation into a shadowed apparition of my dark dreams.

A thud shakes the floor a second before Cain and Declan snap their eyes behind me. A frenzied gasp blasts into me as I spin around, presented with *the maniac*.

"I knew we should've done it my way. We never needed to hide." He advances on me as I back away. In confusion, I glance up, only to see a part of the ceiling taken away.

"Open the gate," Cain demands as he shakes it, rattling my bones as I press my back against the cold metal to stay away from a still approaching Micah.

"I don't think I will." He widens his chilling eyes as he shreds his jacket, letting it fall to the floor as he stalks closer. "Both of you kept me away from *my queen* while you figured out if I was right. But she was waiting for us." As he closes the distance, eating up the space between us with his feral form, he glares his own fury at the men behind me.

Standing less than a foot away from me, he brings his hand to my face. I feel like I should flinch away, but my impulses brutally take over, forcing my body to melt. Someone sees me. *Finally.*

"And I think it's time I punish you all for doubting me. Don't you agree, Baby?" He strokes his thumb across my lips as his gaze lazily travels over my face as if I'm all he needs.

Holding my breath, I rush out everything I need to know before I let my fragile walls crumble for good, no return possible, "If I'm really yours, that means you're mine as well? All of you? Is that what this is? Because…if I'm going to take this insane risk, I won't accept anything short of absolute commitment." I straighten my arms beside me as I tilt my face up to Micah, meaning for that to come out as a question, but it snaps out as a demand.

"Aria…you're everything," Cain murmurs from behind me as he slides his hand through the gate to wrap his fingers around my arm.

"And everything we are…is yours." Declan closes in on the other side of me to drag his blood-stained knuckles over my side. I search my mind and body for the feeling I always have when something gets too real, that need to flee, but it's gone. For the first time, I truly do feel like I belong.

"Then you were right, Micah. Punish us all." I jump in, holding onto this feeling that I would give anything to keep.

Chapter Ten

Aria

"Grab her arms. I don't know if I can hold myself back if her hands are on me," Micah growls his instruction a second before Declan and Cain shove their hands through the gate to secure my arms beside my head.

As Micah's vicious grin pulls up, his knees hit the floor in front of me. My legs are already struggling to hold me up, but when he grabs one of them and slings it over his shoulder, I give most of my weight to the three of them.

I can't even take another breath before he surges his tongue past my wet, waiting pussy. I let out a long, shuddering moan as my head falls back when he starts furiously exploring every inch of me.

Cain and Declan let out maddeningly aggressive grunts from behind me as they spread their fingers out on my exposed skin, brushing over my nipples, digging into my arms, making it feel like the gate is absorbing my burning body.

I shriek as Micah roars against me, wildly working my clit, keeping this dizzying pressure building within me. My muscles tremor in waves, my nerves ravenously ready to explode.

He never lets up his pressure as his two fingers drag through my lips, restarting the pulsing ache inside me. He slides his fingers farther, getting them wet with my arousal. I hold my breath when I realize he's bringing them to my ass.

He continues rolling his tongue against me as his fingers circle and edge into my tight hole, causing my legs to flex and tense around him. As I whine out a moan, my head falls back again as pleasure sparks from my core. When I grind against him, he pushes his fingers in, continuing his slow circles and building a new kind of pressure in my body.

"Holy shit, Aria. I've dreamt of what you'd sound like when we finally got our hands on you…but I wasn't fucking prepared. Make her take it all," Cain groans against my hand as he pulls my fingers through the metal, taking one of them past his lips, tightening my stomach even more.

Micah chuckles harshly against my clit before sucking it past his tongue and surging his fingers into my ass, sending a bolt of lightning through each of my limbs. As he continues his maddening force on me, I gasp and moan for air, focusing on just surviving upright through this. I almost crumble down, but between him holding my hips and the guys trapping my arms, my body stays suspended against the metal.

His pace increases with his force, surging his fingers deep within me as his tongue brutalizes me. As flames burst at the seams within, waves of heat pulse through me as my orgasm does, rolling through my body as my sobbing wail echoes off the walls.

Suddenly, he flies up, forcing me to take my weight back as he crashes his lips to mine again. The guys let my arms go so I can wrap them around Micah's neck, spearing my fingers through his wavy hair and gripping tight as he pulls my hips into him and drags my lip through his teeth. He presses me against the metal as he chokes on a breath and dives to my neck.

"I have to be honest…" I pant out as I drag my nails over his head and raise my leg against him. "I don't really feel punished, *Maniac*." When he pulls back to look at me, his gaze turns savage and I lick my lips as I give him a fiery smirk, wanting him to fucking take me already.

With a snarl, he roughly grabs my hair and forces me to my knees. My hands drag down his stomach, purposefully not touching but getting close to his insane bulge until I hold onto his thighs.

He yanks me back, forcing me to lock eyes with him towering above me. "Before I give you my reigns, I need you to know…you can fight, but I'm still going to fucking take you. You're lucky they're here." He motions to the men behind me as he lowers his voice, but my muscles turn to mush in response. How can something so terrifyingly ominous sound so…romantic. "And you need to understand that we're the only men who are to be trusted with your body. If anyone ever touches you again, they will suffer…" He raises his brows to warn me. "I will not hold back." He grabs my jaw with his other hand, digging his fingers in until my lips part. I nod, not able to speak yet with the amount of hunger rolling through my body.

"You'll still fight us. You fucking *brat*," Cain chuckles as he crouches down and pushes his hand through the gate again to hold my arm, his touch and filthy words feeling like a shot of espresso.

"And she'll love every second of it." Declan does the same as Cain, binding my arms behind me again.

"Eyes on me, Baby. Right now, you're *my* dirty little slut." Micah slaps his hand against my cheek, shooting a bolt of electricity through me. "Now open your fucking mouth and show them how good you take it."

My body works on his command, trapped and his to use. My lips part as he flicks his belt open and pulls out his wide shaft, pouring lava right into my core. My eyes widen at his sheer size before darting up to his glare, everything in me begging for more. I'm done fighting. For now.

When his tip presses against my tongue, I pull against his hand holding my hair to shove him into my mouth. If this is really happening, and they're going to take me out of this dreary existence, then I'm going to show them that they belong to me as well.

I've dreamt of having a partner, someone to have my back, to stand beside me, and to go a little wild with. But I've never felt it. I believed I just didn't connect that way to people.

I didn't know it would feel like this though. It's not shocking, but it's as if I really was waiting for it.

Micah's head falls back with a harsh groan as I wrap my lips around his width and swirl my tongue against his tip. Cain and Declan tighten their grip on me as they curse in frustration, only egging me on more.

As I devour Micah's shaft, reveling in the feel and taste of him against my lips, he uses his grip on my hair to fuck my mouth, hitting the back of my throat to gag me before pulling back and doing it over and over until I'm dizzy from the lack of oxygen and the powerful awakening tearing through me.

"Take it all like the good little whore you are." Cain tightens his grip on my arm with one hand as his other pushes my head down on Micah's cock, slipping his shaft into my throat. He rips my head off Micah, letting me take a filling breath as my core quivers with pressure and heat, forcing me to spread my knees to give my sensitive clit a second to breathe as well.

"More. Give me everything, Micah. Make me your slut." Knowing he and I are torturing the men who are forced to spectate, I lock eyes with Micah who looks more animal than man right now with his shaft in hand.

"Fucking hell," he growls deep in his throat as he uses his grip on my hair to rip me up to stand. Before I know what's happening, he turns me around to shove my face against the metal gate as he yanks my hips back.

Declan doesn't waste a second before pushing his hand through the gate to wrap his fingers around my sore throat. "You're fucking killing me," he grits out as he tightens his grip on the sides of my neck. "But if you don't take her right now, I'm ripping this gate down with my bare hands."

"I was the first to see her, so it's only right that I'm the one who feels her perfect pussy first." Micah slides his shaft through my lips, coating himself in my arousal before lining up to me.

Knowing I'm not going to be eased into this, I hold my breath, but Declan instantly tightens his fingers, cutting off my air. Micah surges inside me at the same time, pushing me up on my toes and digging my cheek into the gate. When Declan releases my throat, I shout out my breath with a sob as my walls are forced to stretch around his shaft.

"We must have done something phenomenal in this life to be redeemed," Micah pants out as he buries himself inside me and holds my hips in his bruising grip. "Because we're in fucking heaven now." As every cell in my body electrifies, he pulls back and rams into me, tearing a scream from my throat.

"Time to rip the cocoon off." Declan tightens his grip again, cutting off any chance of air as Micah slaps his hips against my ass, using his unyielding grip to pull me back to meet his deep, ruthless thrusts.

"Tell me how you killed him…" Micah whips his hand against my ass before snatching my hip to pull me back into him. Snapping his other hand to my hair, he uses it as leverage to ensure every thrust of his shaft slams into the front of my pussy.

"I put pills in his food and kept him starving in the basement while the rats ate away…then I poured gasoline over him…his eyes were open…he felt the flames!" The truth gets torn from my lips, feeling like it's breaking years of stress and resentment from my soul. "He fucking deserved it!"

"That's right, Butterfly," Declan groans deeply as he tightens his grip again, sealing my airways as Micah gyrates his thick cock into me. The pressure inside me aggressively expands, feeling like it's truly ripping me apart.

Just when my head is about to explode from the need for air, Declan releases me, sending electric flames to every limb until nothing else exists. When fingers slide over my clit and furiously circle it, I glance down with a ragged whine to find that its Cain's hand shoved through the gate.

"I was an idiot for not seeing you first," Cain breathes out as he rattles the gate, shaking all of us..

"Tell me how to make you come. I need to feel you fall apart for me." Micah uses his grip on my hair to yank my head back.

"Yes! Just like that! Don't fucking stop," I shout out a moaning wail as I grip the metal gate to help me stay up. The pressure from Micah pounding into me and Cain's fingers on my clit mixed with Declan's manipulation of my air is making every single nerve in my body awake with fire, forcing me towards this excruciatingly powerful eruption.

I try not to move in fear of detonating as Micah hardens his thrusts, pulling all the way back to his tip before slamming inside me, giving me every excruciating inch. The wet sounds of him fucking me into oblivion echo around the empty walls.

Cain quickens his skilled fingers while Declan cuts my air off again, working together to launch my soul off the edge. My muscles tighten in waves as pleasure explodes to every corner when my release rockets through me.

"Fucking right! Yes! Take it all." Micah wraps his arms around me and shoves me against the gate to keep me standing as he continues his brutal pace inside me, forcing his cock past my spasming walls. Declan releases me again, letting me exhale and scream out in bliss, my voice beating off every wall.

"Holy…shit!" I cry out as my orgasm won't stop when Micah won't either, letting my trembling feet dangle just off the floor as he holds me up. I can barely take it!

"I swear to God, I will shoot you if this gate does not open." Declan rips a gun out from his holster on his side and points it right at Micah who furiously slams into me, groaning on every breath, seemingly unaware of the danger being presented to him.

"I can take another bullet. I'm not stopping until my cum is dripping out of her. You want that? You want me to fill you?" Micah raggedly pants out as he grabs my jaw and forces my face back to him. I nod without another thought, wanting everything. All of them! *Fuck yes!*

My body viciously convulses with my unbearable release as danger lurks around every inch. Micah suddenly takes a few steps back and falls onto the table, dragging me with him. With a harsh roar, he coils his arms around my middle and chest to hold me tight, forcing me to sit on top of him with his cock buried deep within me, swelling with his release.

I grab his forearms as my head falls back onto his shoulder, my legs quivering up as my muscles shudder with the aftershocks of the most powerful orgasm I've ever had. When I pry my eyes open, a blast of fear makes me instantly needy for more as I truly absorb the deadly visage of Declan pointing his gun at Micah's head, his glare burning with fury. *Quite a gift indeed.*

When Micah kisses my neck as his cock swells again, truly filling me, a shiver crawls up my spine, fluttering my eyes closed. They snap open when I realize Cain is storming towards us with a metal garbage can raised over his head.

The blast that goes off when he slams it against the lock shakes me to my core. The gate is ripped open by the two of them, looking furiously powerful as they approach me.

"Are you ready for more, Butterfly?" Declan steps towards me and taps the barrel of his gun under my chin to raise me up.

"Make me yours," I whisper my plea, sealing my fate with them.

Chapter Eleven
Aria

Declan takes charge, not wasting a second before putting his shoulder into my middle and throwing me over his back. I shriek when Micah's cock is pulled out of me, but Declan slides his hand gently through my lips, distracting me from the sting and rising my greed for more.

"I watched you for weeks, bouncing around this display. Your tempting body and wicked glare pulling me in more every minute." Declan storms towards the Christmas tree in the center of the mall. "I thought for a few months that we should leave you be, but I've still been picturing every filthy thing I wanted to do to you all year."

As I brace myself on his back, letting his sinful words fill my body with heat, tears start forming in my eyes again. This year, I never wanted to leave. I couldn't figure out why, but I didn't have the same desire to run. But I think it's because they were surrounding me. I finally felt safe.

Micah runs past us with a lewd laugh as I watch Cain's boots hitting the floor right behind Declan. "Working with you was my last-ditch effort to see if you really wanted us. Every day I saw what was between us." Cain grips my hair to bring my face up to him, both of them still storming me towards the display.

"This is fucking crazy. But…I wanted you. I *want* all of you," I let out a breathless moan as Declan continues gently rubbing my arousal and Micah's cum around my pussy.

As Declan drops me to the ground and grabs my face, he presses his lips against mine and slides his hands into my hair before I can take a breath. His tongue swirls with mine as we coil our arms around each other.

"You'll always have us, Butterfly," he whispers his promise as he breaks the kiss, forcing another tear from my eye.

He spins me around, gripping my arms to keep me steady. My eyes blow wide open when I'm presented with the lit-up Christmas display. The tree is gorgeously ablaze with color, surrounded by the melting candles, spreading a warm glow to only us, as if we're all that exists in this moment.

As I stare at the emblems I've only ever associated with my resentment towards this cruel holiday, it's like it's the first time I'm seeing it. No bitterness, no waiting for the hatred, just…magic.

Cain slides around us to stand between me and Santa's chair behind him. "You've spent enough time on your own." His words are soft, but when he snatches my neck and yanks me forward, I know he's ready to introduce himself.

As he shoves me into the wide, burgundy chair, the air gets jolted out of me as all three of them stand above me, glaring at me like wolves about to feast on their next meal. Working only on impulse, I reach behind me and unclasp my bra before throwing it away. Their gaze turns voracious as I bare myself to them, scars and all.

"Where the fuck have you been hiding?" Micah murmurs as he stomps to the side and grips the arm of the chair, his lips twitching like he's barely holding himself back.

"I'm sure she'll love torturing us for taking so long to find her." Declan stands on the other side and leans his elbows down on the arm of the chair like he's getting ready to watch a show.

"I want your eyes on me." Cain taps his boot against the side of my foot to make me spread my legs, pulling my focus.

My heart pounds against my ribs again as he slides the suspenders off his shoulders, letting his stiff cock rest against his abdomen. I have absolutely no idea what happens tomorrow, but I know I'll be spending Christmas sore and sated.

Cain drops his pants to the ground before ripping off his shirt, showing me every inch of his lean, deadly frame. His sporadic wounds that are mixed with his ink are a testament to the hard life I think they've lived. I want to know everything. No secrets.

When he drops to one knee, I lean up to touch him, but he yanks my hips forward, forcing me to brace myself on my elbows as my breathing picks up. He glides his hand up my stomach before brushing between my breasts and urging my head to fallback. When he slides the tip of his cock through my drenched lips, I close my eyes in preparation, but his hand slides to my jaw to tilt my face down.

"Watch your pussy take every inch," he murmurs softly as he slips inside of me. I take in a quick breath as my knees hike up around him, but he eases inside me, only giving me an inch at a time before pulling back.

As we watch his thick cock surge inside of me, his soft lips part as the muscles across his chest tighten. He slowly pushes forward, sensually gyrating his hips against me. I tilt my head over to Micah when his panting turns ragged, showing his impatience to watch me be fucked hard.

When I look over to Declan, he crouches down and rests his chin on his folded arms to bore his gaze into every move we make as if we're the greatest show he's ever seen. I slide my hand around Cain's bicep as he trails his fingers up my thighs, our hips rolling against each other like we've been preparing for this show all year.

He hooks his arm around the back of my thigh to spread my legs around him as he locks eyes with me, hitting a deeper part of me while gazing into my eyes.

"I'll never hide again," I whisper as I trail my hands up his firm chest, causing a guttural rumble to escape each of them. "I want to be the only thing you see." I drag my tongue across my bottom lip, knowing he's about to kiss me again. As he molds his chest to mine, we wrap our arms around each other, continuing the torment of Micah and Declan which is officially my new favorite hobby.

As Cain raises up, he gives me a devious smirk like he knows what I'm thinking. He stretches both my legs up to rest against his chest as he stays deep inside me for a moment.

"I think I want to see her in a little more red," Cain muses as he gives Declan and Micah the same smirk. Not knowing if that means blood or not, I simply wait for my next gift, my eyes rolling from the charged pressure building inside me.

Micah slides his fingers into mine to stretch my arm so he can press his lips against my knuckles. Declan does the same with my other hand, pulling my arm out to the side which makes me fall onto my back.

Cain circles his hips, staying deep within me and constricting my air as the other two start wrapping the thick red ribbon from the chair around my wrists. A giggle almost escapes me at their soft, coordinated movements, but it's replaced by a shriek when Cain pulls back and slams into me.

"Now you're all mine," he growls harshly as he bands an arm around my thighs and rocks his hips against me, not giving me a second to get used to his vicious pace.

My muscles tightening from the brutal sensations, I try to pull my arms in, but the guys have them tied and secured in their unyielding grip. Micah's taunting laugh breaks through the blood rushing through my ears as my head gets thrown back from the force of Cain's thrusts.

Cain bends my knees into my chest, tilting my hips and allowing him to hit the deepest parts of me, shoving my air out of me until I'm gasping and wailing on each breath. The pressure inside me starts expanding my skin more on each thrust.

"That's my good little whore, taking my cock so fucking well," Cain grounds out as he whips the side of my thigh, sending a shockwave through me that has me wanting to cry out for more, but no words can form on my tongue, no coherent thoughts rooting in my mind.

"Oh, I think she likes that, boys," Micah chuckles darkly as he reaches over to slide his hand across my stinging skin.

86

"Of course she fucking does." Declan moves in behind the chair, pulling my arm with him. Even though my eyes fight to stay closed under the onslaught of sensations, I desperately try to pry them open, not knowing who to look at first.

"Jesus Christ, your pussy is going to be the death of me," Cain groans out as he grabs the back of the chair to give his thrusts even more power, sending tremors through my limbs as he pushes against every nerve inside me.

"Fuck!" I cry out as he slams inside me, making it feel like I'm being torn apart and put back together quicker than I can keep up. I howl out again when Micah whips his hand on the underside of my breast. He bares his teeth and laughs when I try to pull my arms back in to cover myself. "You fucking assholes," I moan out as my chest arches off the couch, their manipulations of my body making it feel like I have no control over myself at all. They truly own me in this moment.

When I fight back, the wild energy from all three of them seems to ignite the air around us.

"I want to wreck you, Aria…make you only fit us," Cain pants out and hardens his pace when I shove my legs against him.

"I think our girl wants to be fucking taken," Declan growls deep in his throat as he rounds the couch again. All three of them let out a merciless laugh before I realize what they're doing.

A shriek gets pulled from me when Cain flips us around, grabbing my legs to make me straddle him as he leans back on the chair. He grabs my face before slamming his lips to mine and grinding up into me. Again, I pull my arms, but Micah and Declan quickly secure the ribbon that binds them behind my back.

"There's no getting out of this now, my love. Your mind, your soul, and this body…all belong to us," Cain whispers as he holds the back of my head, his grip tightening on my hair.

"You don't…" I go to snap back at him, but I'm yanked up by Declan, plastering my back against his front.

"Don't you dare finish that," Declan snarls against my ear as he pushes me down on Cain's cock so I have to take every inch. "You can fight, but you will *not* lie to us. Ever. You are ours." His rough tone sends a quake through each of my muscles, causing even Cain to groan as he grips my hips and holds me down on his thick shaft.

"That's all I want." I give myself over to them, not knowing if being conquered or worshipped turns me on more, but I'm about to explode. *Holy shit.*

The ragged breath that escapes Declan spreads desire and heat over my neck, my declaration affecting his entire body.

"Such a good fucking girl," he breathes out before snapping his grip from my hair to my tied arms, keeping me suspended over Cain. As I grind on top of him, I look back at Declan as he grabs a small tube from his pocket.

As the candlelight flickers against his ominous frame and the dark ink covering his arms and neck, he starts looking more phantom than man, which makes me want him more every second. Why be afraid of anything when I have a demon at my back?

When he bites down on the top of the tube to tear the cap off, I finally realize it's lube. He came prepared.

"You ready to be filled, Baby?" Micah leans over the back of the couch and grabs my jaw to pull me over to him. I'm poised over Cain as he holds my hips and Micah grasps my jaw, bringing his lips a breath away from mine. "I want to watch as Declan stretches your tight ass. I want to sit front fucking row as I watch the pain make you come harder than you ever have."

I take in a quick breath followed by a ragged moan when Declan slides two fingers into my ass, spreading the lube over me. As he grabs my hips to pull me back into him, Cain's shaft slips out a moment before Declan slides his own into my waiting pussy. His body shudders as he curses out a slew of rough praises while gyrating his hips against me, letting me get used to this new fullness that's stealing my air.

"Holy shit. I can't…" I breathe out as the pressure inside me starts to feel like it's constricting my organs.

"There's nothing you can't do." Cain brings his face to my chest as his hands slide up my sides. While stroking his wet shaft between us, he leaves demanding kisses along my breasts, dragging his teeth across my nipples, forcing even more sensations into my overwhelmed body.

My eyes keep rolling as Declan thrusts into me from behind, expertly gliding his cock against the front of my pussy while twisting and curling his fingers inside my ass.

"You were made for us. Your body already knows it. And you're going to fucking take it. Understood?" Declan grits as he slides a third finger into my ass.

"Take me, Sir. Give me everything. Now." On my plea, I shove my hips back against him, sending a coursing shudder into all three of them. With a dark chuckle, Declan pulls out of my pussy, only to be quickly replaced by Cain who pulls me down onto him, keeping my body flooded with them, filled exactly how I crave.

"There she is," Micah hisses a second before crushing his lips to me again, sliding his tongue to meet mine and groaning roughly against me.

I cry into him as Declan replaces his fingers with the wide, tapered head of his cock. Cain slows his thrusts a bit, focusing on brushing his lips, teeth, and tongue over my breasts, probably to distract me from the unbearable expanding sensation that being filled like this brings.

Micah and I breathe in each other's air as he holds my face gazes into my shattering soul. Declan curses under his breath as he glides his agonizing cock into my ass, stretching me around him.

"I can feel you inside her. Holding back is fucking torture. Micah was right," Cain snarls against my skin before digging his teeth into the side of my breast.

"Be patient. It won't be long before we're begging her for mercy," Declan breathes out as he gives me another few inches, my body not feeling like it can keep up.

"Oh, fuck! I...it's...shit!" I stumble and choke over my words as the air burns in my lungs. Micah quietly coos against me as he trails his lips down my neck to soothe me, all three of them gently getting me used to them.

Declan's hands curl around my tied arms behind me, his fingers digging into my skin. When his hips sit against my ass, neither of them move for a second, forcing my body to take each and every inch of them. I gasp for air as I tremble furiously between them all.

"Fuck, you're perfect," Declan yanks me away from Micah, trapping my tied arms between us. He wraps his hand against my neck and dives his mouth to my throat as he starts slowly grinding within me.

On each breath I cry in agony, and each exhale, I moan for more as Declan and Cain move in a constant rhythm, never letting me be empty, filling me beyond reason.

Cain lays back down again and holds my sides to guide my movements as Declan circles his hips against my ass, both of them letting out maddeningly rough groans as my walls quiver around them. When Micah flips over the back of the chair to stand on the seat over Cain, already holding his rigid cock in his hand, Declan grabs my hair again to force my face to the front as Micah frames my jaw.

As Cain and Declan roll our bodies together, building the pulsing detonation inside me, I can only focus on breathing, knowing I won't survive my next orgasm, but I'm ready to leave this world with a fucking bang.

"Open your mouth and choke on me." Micah's lips twitch up in a snarl as he digs his fingers into my jaw and tightens his grip on the base of his cock.

I can still only obey as I part my lips and slide my tongue out. As Micah thrusts into my mouth, Declan shoves me forward, pushing Micah's cock into my throat. When I gag, my entire body tenses around Cain and Declan's shafts, inciting a violent thunder out of them as they harden their pace, blasting my skin off my sweltering bones.

Micah's head falls back as he holds my face and thrusts his cock into my mouth. The feel of him sliding against me, controlling my breath and being completely at his mercy sends bolts of lightning straight to my core on every thrust.

The four of us become one, a flurry of sweaty skin, demanding hands, pulsing heat, and wet, guttural noises that these empty walls have never seen.

A blast of fire hits me without warning when Declan trails his hand around me and slides his fingers over my sensitive clit. The fireball rips and ravages my muscles so profoundly that I can barely register that I'm coming. My orgasm blurs the lines of consciousness as I writhe in pleasure.

A pounding beat in my ears dulls the sounds around me, only letting their filthy words through, blending into a melody.

"Come on my fucking cock, my little whore."

"Look at you come...you're fucking incredible."

"You take it so well, Baby."

"Beg us to fill you," Declan's demand finally pulls me out of my dark hazy bliss of an orgasm, but another one is barreling straight for me, my used muscles already tensing in preparation. Micah steals my words by shoving his cock against my throat, quickening his pace, and forcing my lips to spread around him.

I whine against his cock for them to fill me, feeling like it's all I want. I've been empty my whole life. Oh...*wow*. My orgasm doesn't roll into me this time, instead destroying me as a nuclear explosion rips apart my entire being, pulling my muscles as taut as they can go, lighting every single nerve in my body.

When I can't hold down my scream, Micah pulls out of my mouth and furiously strokes his cock in front of my face as Declan holds me against him, he and Cain still brutally thrusting past my clenching walls. I bellow out my liberation, screaming every dark thing that's left inside of me, only leaving room for them.

Time loses all sense of meaning as Declan slams me down on top of Cain who wraps his arms around me and buries his cock deep inside my walls. My mind blurs again, the exhaustion of my entire life catching up with me, finally easing me under now that I'm safe.

I can feel them all panting and groaning, maybe even yelling, but I can't hear anything. As hands hold onto me from every direction, all I hear is the slight ringing of Christmas bells drifting me off into sleep.

Magic.

Chapter Twelve
Declan

She passed out within seconds of her last orgasm. I figured she would. She's strong, but a body can only take so much.

Carrying her to our truck wasn't the issue, it was calming Micah down when he couldn't wake her. This last year has been hard to restrain him, and I can't hold him back any longer. Only she can.

He's currently laying in the backseat with her sleeping on top of him, softly telling her stories about our lives. Things we haven't spoken about in years.

About how his parents raised him in a meth trailer and used him to peddle their product. And about how Cain's mother used him as currency to supply her own addiction. And how my father whipped me every single day to keep me obedient.

Our life would have consumed us if we didn't have each other, but none of the evil bastards surrounding us were prepared for the three of us to join together. And they weren't ready when we decided we'd had enough and showed up to slaughter them.

After the three of us survived our killing spree that we thought was a suicide mission, we decided being locked up wasn't going to be our future. We had to be smart. Micah was going to end up overdosing or in a padded room, Cain was ready to end it all, and I wanted to slice into every person I met. But we were bonded in violence.

We swore we'd always stay together, become a unit. Our work is bloody but effective, nailing home whatever point the client wants to make. We've made a small name for ourselves in the criminal underworld, but our lives are empty. Never in my wildest dreams did I think we would find someone to join us.

All of us ended up killing the people who were supposed to look out for us, just like Aria did. She went through hell, but still lived easily amongst average people. We can't do that. And I knew if we drug her down with us, she wouldn't be able to live normally again.

Unfortunately for her, I'm a selfish prick. I knew months ago there was no way she'd get away from us. Wherever she goes, we'll follow. And if she wants us not to kill for money…actually, I'm not even going to entertain that possibility. She'll see the scum we get hired to snuff out, and she'll revel in their destruction. I know that now.

As Cain drives with the first real smile I've seen on his face in years, not the fake one he shows to the outside world, he hums a low tune. He's the face of our group, being the one to interact with people because he's the one with the best mask.

No one feels that comfortable around Micah or me, but these past few weeks that Cain has been able to be around her and be shown the kind of acceptance and esteem that Aria subconsciously already feels for us, I've never seen him need his mask less.

"What are you thinking?" Cain asks without taking his eyes off the dark, snowy road ahead of us.

"The fact that without knowing it, without changing anything about herself, she's made us all…happy. I don't think I've felt that before." I lean my elbow on the middle console as I close my eyes, enjoying the fact that the truck smells like her. Her sweat, her arousal, and her blood.

"It's love, Declan." Cain keeps his voice low as he glances back at her for a moment. She's still sleeping, softly snoring against his chest, but he can't wait for her to know everything. We'll have plenty of time for that.

"Where are we?" she mutters as she rubs her eyes with her fist. Micah gasps as a wide grin takes over his face before he tugs more blankets over her naked body.

"Wherever you want to go, my love." Cain glances back at her again.

She props up on Micah's chest as she looks around in confusion, a small smile on her face remaining. "I don't care," she snorts back a laugh like those words surprised her. "Just…as long as I'm here." Her lips tremble as she looks at each of us, her soft, soulful eyes telling me everything I need to know. She might not understand it yet, but she loves us too.

"We'll always be here. Let us take care of everything for a while." I reach back to wipe a tear from her cheek, letting her eyes close in contentment. She's been worried her entire life, and no one deserves a break more than she does. As she lays back down on Micah and he coils his arms around her again, all of us relax as peace spreads to each of us.

"Merry fucking Christmas."

Chapter Thirteen

Cain

Two years later

"I'm going to rip his eyes out for looking at you like this! Pull off each of his fingers for touching you..." Micah's snarls at Aria through the radio to her earpiece as he paces around the hotel room, glaring at the video feed we have of the restaurant downstairs where she's on a date with our target.

My lips pull up when I see the moment she hears Micah. She lets her eyes close for a moment as she crosses her legs, leaning even closer to our target. She better hurry up because I'm ready to storm in there with Micah.

She's taking her time with this one, probably because she knows how sick he really is. How deserving of agony he is. How many innocents he's hurt. She jumped at the chance to help with this job.

When she throws her head back with a laugh, she slaps his chest and trails her hand over his shoulder, knowing the more she touches him, the more he suffers. As he leans into whisper against her ear, her eyes dart to the camera she knows we're using as her menacing smirk pulls to the side.

Fuck, she's perfect.

She gracefully gets up and slips her hand into the crux of his elbow as he leads the way to the elevators. Micah starts tucking some of his curved blades into his holster as he hums the tune Aria sings when they cook together.

Declan shakes his head with a grin as the two of them slip around the corner of the suite to stay hidden. In the past, we would simply bombard our target, shock and pain right off the bat. But since Aria's been doing jobs with us, she's started getting us to be a bit more delicate. She says there's something inherently disturbing about a quiet introduction to the end of their lives. She believes they deserve to know they had a chance to get away.

The three of us may be violent, ruthless, and brutal, but she's as clever as she is cruel. She's led us from a small-time group that took odd jobs whenever we needed money, to a major player in the underworld, being hired to take out more powerful targets all the time.

She may be our Queen, but she's well on her way to being the boss soon. She's still our little brat though.

As our target's vile, suggestive tone filters through the door, a low snarl comes from Micah who's still tucked away. I straighten out my suit as I get ready for her.

Now that we have money to burn, I learned I have quite expensive tastes. It's more than the three of us showering Aria in anything she desires, but we dress like we belong with the rich assholes we take out now. I've moved past wearing cheap Santa costumes, and now have an entire closet filled with three-piece, tailored suits. The boy I was, wouldn't recognize the man I've become.

"Tell me again…what do you want with me?" Aria's smooth voice curls around me as she walks backwards into the room, holding onto our target's tie to coax him to follow her, her swaying hips and tempting gaze hypnotizing him.

She's so dangerously alluring that he doesn't even see me leaning against the back of the couch. Or the chair we've placed in the middle of the room with zip ties for his limbs. We've given him plenty of chances to realize he's in peril.

"Don't worry, Baby. I'll be taking what I want. You're in for a hell of a night." The target lets out a low, suggestive laugh as he flicks open the button on his pants.

"I was just about to say that to you, my friend." As I finally pipe up, a giggle rises out of Aria as our target's eyes snap to me.

"I was thinking the same thing." She winks at me from over her shoulder, pulling my grin wide in return. He glances from me to her as his brows pinch in, the two of us pulling his focus enough for Declan and Micah to slip in behind him and stand by the door. And just like that, his chances of escaping are gone.

"What the fuck is going on here? He your pimp?" He slaps her hands off his tie as his sweaty face starts turning red. As her heels snap off the floors, her soft laughter turns frightening as she keeps sauntering backwards, pulling her sexy, green cocktail dress taut over her curved frame.

"I wouldn't worry too much about *him*," she sighs quietly as she presses back against me, my hands sliding over her hips in reaction.

"You're about to meet the only man allowed to call her *baby*," Micah growls harshly as he launches himself at the target before he's even turned around, crushing his fist right into the middle of his spine. He cries out in pain as he crumples to the ground, about to experience the worst night of his life, starting with a few broken ribs.

He screams and cries for mercy as Micah and Declan roughly tie him to the chair, but my love doesn't let me go and help yet. She keeps her back plastered against my front as her hands cover my own to lead them to her breasts. She'll never have to ask me twice. Diving my mouth to her exposed neck, I ravish her skin and dig my fingers into her.

"What the fuck?" Micah shouts his protests a second before a guttural scream is ripped from our target.

"What are you doing?" Declan storms over and grabs her jaw to tilt her up to him as she rolls her body against mine. "We have work to do, and this man does not deserve to see you like this." He scowls down at her, and in response, she kicks off her heels and grabs my hand to shove it between her legs. *Fuck yes.*

I never stop my mouth from devouring her skin as my fingers slide through her pussy. "No underwear? You bad fucking girl." I slap my hand against her clit, sending a jolt through her frame as she lets out a soft moan.

Declan shakes his head as he clicks his tongue off his teeth to scold her. He actually thinks that's effective to make her want to obey him, but I can practically feel her temperature rising in response as she feeds off defying him. He brings his face closer to her as he tilts her up to him. "Answer me. Or I will…"

"What are you going to do, Sir?" she snaps at him, never stopping her body from grinding against me, driving me fucking wild. "You have work to do, so get the information the client is asking for, and then make that sick piece of shit pay." She grabs the front of his shirt before going up on her tiptoes to bring her face closer to his. I follow every step, trapping her between us. "And make it quick…because Cain has me all to himself until you're done. Did you hear that, my maniac?" She lets go of Declan to wrap her arm back around my neck as she calls to Micah.

"You'll see how fast I can beg him to end it, Baby. And then you're *mine*." A second after Micah snarls out his devotion to her, an agonizing cry explodes from the target before Micah muzzles him.

"You'll pay for this, Butterfly." Declan brushes his thumb across her lips as he gives her a heated, threatening grin.

"I can't wait." She drags her tongue across her teeth as she lifts her legs around his, but he backs away as his eyes narrow.

A harsh laugh gets shoved out of me as I rip her dress down her arms to bare her body for us. Micah gives her a snarling laugh before taking out our target's eyes. At least the last thing he got to see was a goddess. That's all the three of us can hope for in this life.

"I love you, Cain," she whispers as she turns her face up to me. My movements stop in an instant as my heart constricts in my chest to the point of breaking.

"Are you serious?" The words shudder out of me as I spin her around and grab her face. She nods as a tear slips out of her eye, and I worriedly glance behind her at the guys, knowing we're in for a fucking ride if they heard her.

"Don't worry about them. I already told them how I feel. I saved you for last." She slides her hands up my torso as crimson spreads over her chest.

"You know I love you." I don't phrase it as a question because I already know the answer. I've been telling her since I first spoke to her.

"I know. I've never said those words before though. I'm really impressed with how patient you all have been." She wraps her arms around my neck as I coil mine around her middle, sliding down to grip her ass. It actually hasn't been easy. She took way longer than we thought, but she shows us every day how she feels, and…

"It got easier to wait because you started saying it in your sleep so long ago," I let out an amused breath as I place kisses up her neck.

She drops her head back with a musical laugh. "Yeah, Micah showed me the recording he has of me. You assholes." As she slaps my chest, I quickly grab her hand to continue trailing my lips up her arm, the two of us in a picturesque moment alone while Declan and Cain rip apart our target.

"You told Micah first, didn't you?" I can't help but feel that animal inside me pounding in my chest again, but he's much quieter now. It helps that there's nothing better in this world than her being happy. Actually, watching her come is *otherworldly*. And between the three of us, she's never left wanting. I couldn't keep up with her on my own. My body is strong, but I was right, she needs all of us.

"I did. And I made sure we were in a safe area, without weapons or other people. You'd have been impressed," she chuckles out as she slips her hands to my belt. "And I kept you for last because you teased me for weeks…and I've never gotten back at you."

"I waited months for you." I roughly grab her jaw, not stopping her movements around my belt at all, loving when she gets this *starving* glint in her eyes.

"Every action deserves an equal consequence. Don't you agree?" she quotes Declan as she slips her hands into my pants to frame my cock with her delicate fingers. Digging my teeth into my lip, I nod, ready for any punishment she can think of as long as her hands stay on me. "Don't come until I say so…understood?" She slides her tongue out to wet her lip, her sultry tone making my skin seem to burn through my clothes. The crimson on her flushed skin morphs with her auburn hair, turning her into the devilish goddess I know she is.

"Anything you say, my love." At my words, she slides to the ground, already wrapping her mouth around my cock before her knees touch the floor, her confidence soaring as she flexes her power over me. "Fucking hell," I choke on my groan as I spear my fingers through her hair and drop my head back.

Forcing my eyes to stay open, I revel in the power of watching Micah and Declan take out their fury on our target until he's begging for death while my love brings me to the brink over and over.

The four of us were given nothing, treated like vermin and sacrificed to the evil of this world. But together, with her, nothing will keep us down again.

Thank you so much for reading!

I can't thank you enough for giving my smutty little Christmas tales a chance. They were fun and hot to write, so I hope they were a little holiday treat for you.

A special thank you to my beta readers and my editor.

If you have a minute, I'd appreciate it more than you know if you left a review. It's something that truly helps authors. Also, if you enjoyed my writing, or the smut got your heart pumping, I have other, much longer stories available on amazon and kindle unlimited.

Website - **shelbymanuel.com**

TikTok & Instagram s.e.m.writer

Facebook Book club - Shelby's Dark Romance Readers